THE EDENBOURG TATTLER

June 2001

Word has it that Edenbourg's beloved—and oh-so-private—**Princess Isabel Stanbury** is off on a secret mission to rescue her missing father with the help of the only man she's ever truly loved. It seems she and her former commanding officer, **Adam Sinclair**—could he possibly look any better in his royal navy uniform?—are posing as a married couple in order to infiltrate the group suspected of kidnapping the king. But from what my sources tell me, these two might not be *feigning* wedded bliss, because their true feelings *aren't* part of the act! The question is, just when will they realize they've stopped pretending?

Dear Reader,

This June—traditionally the month of brides, weddings and the promise of love everlasting—Silhouette Romance also brings you the possibility of being a star! Check out the details of this special promotion in each of the six happily-ever-afters we have for you.

In *An Officer and a Princess*, Carla Cassidy's suspenseful conclusion to the bestselling series ROYALLY WED: THE STANBURYS, Princess Isabel calls on her former commanding officer to help rescue her missing father. Karen Rose Smith delights us with a struggling mom who refuses to fall for *Her Tycoon Boss* until the dynamic millionaire turns up the heat! In *A Child for Cade* by reader favorite Patricia Thayer, Cade Randall finds that his first love has kept a precious secret from him....

Talented author Alice Sharpe's latest offering, *The Baby Season*, tells of a dedicated career woman tempted by marriage and motherhood with a rugged rancher and his daughter. In *Blind-Date Bride*, the second book of Myrna Mackenzie's charming twin duo, the heroine asks a playboy billionaire to ward off the men sent by her matchmaking brothers. And a single mom decides to tell the man she has always loved that he has a son in Belinda Barnes's heartwarming tale, *The Littlest Wrangler*.

Next month be sure to return for two brand-new series— the exciting DESTINY, TEXAS by Teresa Southwick and the charming THE WEDDING LEGACY by Cara Colter. And don't forget the triumphant conclusion to Patricia Thayer's THE TEXAS BROTHERHOOD, along with three more wonderful stories!

Happy Reading!

Mary-Theresa Hussey

Mary-Theresa Hussey
Senior Editor

Please address questions and book requests to:
Silhouette Reader Service
U.S.: 3010 Walden Ave., P.O. Box 1325, Buffalo, NY 14269
Canadian: P.O. Box 609, Fort Erie, Ont. L2A 5X3

An Officer
and a Princess

CARLA CASSIDY

SILHOUETTE *Romance*

Published by Silhouette Books

America's Publisher of Contemporary Romance

To Judy Christenberry, who shares the angst of every word
written in all of my books, and the joys and angst of my life, as well.
I'm fairly certain we are sisters who were separated at birth,
and I'm grateful fate brought us together again!

Special thanks and acknowledgment are given to Carla Cassidy for her
contribution to the ROYALLY WED: THE STANBURYS series.

 SILHOUETTE BOOKS

ISBN 0-373-19522-2

AN OFFICER AND A PRINCESS

Copyright © 2001 by Harlequin Books S.A.

All rights reserved. Except for use in any review, the reproduction
or utilization of this work in whole or in part in any form by any
electronic, mechanical or other means, now known or hereafter
invented, including xerography, photocopying and recording, or in
any information storage or retrieval system, is forbidden without
the written permission of the editorial office, Silhouette Books,
300 East 42nd Street, New York, NY 10017 U.S.A.

All characters in this book have no existence outside the imagination of
the author and have no relation whatsoever to anyone bearing the same
name or names. They are not even distantly inspired by any individual
known or unknown to the author, and all incidents are pure invention.

This edition published by arrangement with Harlequin Books S.A.

® and TM are trademarks of Harlequin Books S.A., used under license.
Trademarks indicated with ® are registered in the United States Patent
and Trademark Office, the Canadian Trade Marks Office and in other
countries.

Visit Silhouette at www.eHarlequin.com

Printed in U.S.A.

Books by Carla Cassidy

CARLA CASSIDY

is an award-winning author who has written over thirty-five books for Silhouette. In 1995 she won Best Silhouette Romance from *Romantic Times Magazine* for *Anything for Danny*. In 1998 she also won a Career Achievement Award from *Romantic Times Magazine* for Best Innovative Series.

Carla believes the only thing better than curling up with a good book to read is sitting down at the computer with a good story to write. She's looking forward to writing many more books and bringing hours of pleasure to readers.

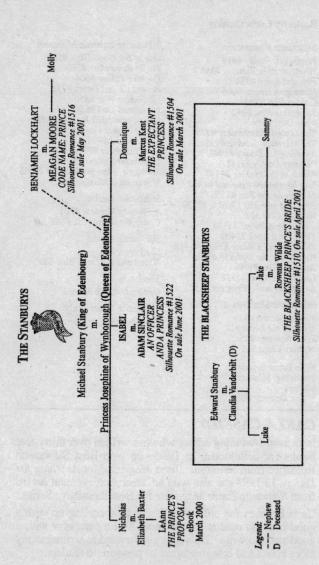

THE STANBURYS

Michael Stanbury (King of Edenbourg)
m.
Princess Josephine of Wynborough (Queen of Edenbourg)

BENJAMIN LOCKHART
m.
MEAGAN MOORE
CODE NAME: PRINCE
Silhouette Romance #1516
On sale May 2001
— Molly

ISABEL
m.
ADAM SINCLAIR
*AN OFFICER
AND A PRINCESS*
Silhouette Romance #1522
On sale June 2001

Dominique
m.
Marcus Kent
*THE EXPECTANT
PRINCESS*
Silhouette Romance #1504
On sale March 2001

Nicholas
m.
Elizabeth Baxter
*THE PRINCE'S
PROPOSAL*
eBook
March 2000

THE BLACKSHEEP STANBURYS

Edward Stanbury
m.
Claudia Vanderbilt (D)

Luke

Jake
m.
Rowena Wilde
THE BLACKSHEEP PRINCE'S BRIDE
Silhouette Romance #1510, On sale April 2001

LeAnn

Sammy

Legend:
- - - Nephew
D — Deceased

Chapter One

Lieutenant Commander Adam Sinclair hated waiting.

He glanced at his watch and frowned, staring at the door that would eventually open to allow him entry into her office.

Her. Isabel Stanbury. Not only a Princess of Edenbourg, but also a cabinet member and on the staff of the Ministry of Defense, and the woman who never seemed to drift far from his thoughts…a woman he could never, ever have as his own except in the forbidden dreams he had far too frequently.

Although he'd only been waiting a little over ten minutes, this wait seemed longer, more difficult than usual as he remembered her voice on the phone when she'd set up this appointment.

She'd sounded agitated, excited, and that worried him. Isabel was a strong woman who rarely gave in to her emotions, but she'd definitely sounded emotional on the phone.

His frown deepened, and he fought the impulse to rise and pace the small confines of the waiting room. Isabel's secretary looked up, as if sensing his impatience, but she offered no reassuring smile.

Smiles were in short supply in Edenbourg these days. Three months ago King Michael had been kidnapped, throwing the entire small country into chaos. Since that time, Michael's son, Crown Prince Nicholas was in hiding but presumed dead by the country as part of the royal plan, and Edward Stanbury, Michael's estranged brother, had become King of Edenbourg. In other words, things in the country were in a royal mess.

Adam had been away at the time of the king's kidnapping, working on a mission of his own...trying to clear his father's name. But, he'd put his personal goals on hold when Isabel had called him home to aid in the search for the missing King Michael.

And that's what they'd been doing for the past two months...following leads, investigating friends and family...and hitting the eventual dead ends.

"Lieutenant Sinclair," the secretary called to him. "You can go in now."

Adam nodded, stood and straightened his uniform jacket. He knew he was the epitome of a well-groomed officer. No errant pieces of lint spotted his pristine uniform, nor did a single dark hair stray from his close-cropped style. He knew what was expected from a high-ranking member of the Royal Edenbourg Navy, and Adam worked double-time to see that he not only met but surpassed expectations.

He had to work double time. He had to overcome the whispered rumors, the veiled innuendoes about his father. He shoved this painful thought aside as he opened the door to the office.

Isabel rose from behind her desk as he walked in. He stopped in the doorway and offered her a crisp salute.

"Lieutenant Sinclair," she greeted him in that deep, low voice that he'd always found far too attractive. "Please, close the door behind you and have a seat." She gestured to the chair in front of her desk.

He closed the door, then sat, trying not to notice how lovely she looked. As usual she was dressed in a smart blue business suit, the ornate family crest decorating one breast pocket.

What was unusual was the careless disarray of her shoulder-length dark brown hair and the bruise-like smudges of dark circles beneath her gorgeous green eyes. Both gave her an uncharacteristic vulnerability.

She looked tired and edgy, and an answering edginess stirred inside him.

He knew the past three months had been difficult on her. Although she and her father had often not seen eye to eye on her place in the royal family, he knew of her enormous love for King Michael.

She didn't sit, but rather moved to the front of the desk and leaned back against it, displaying to him the perfect slender shapeliness of her long legs beneath the short, pencil-thin skirt. The thought of those legs of hers had given Adam many a sleepless night.

Princess Isabel Stanbury was not pretty in the traditional sense although there was beauty in her strong, bold features. Dark brows arched above the greenest eyes he'd ever seen. Her nose was narrow and straight…the Stanbury nose. Her mouth was generous, slightly too big for her face until she smiled, then it seemed to fit perfectly well.

"Thank you for coming," she said. As always the air crackled with tension between them. "There have been some new developments."

He leaned forward, intrigued by any news that might help in their search. "What kind of new developments?"

The last "developments" she'd pursued had nearly gotten her killed. Adam worked to control a shudder as he thought of how close she had come to getting a bullet in her back.

She reached to the desktop behind her, the slight stretch causing her jacket to pull taut across her breasts. Adam felt as if the temperature in the room had climbed a full ten degrees.

He averted his gaze to the wall to her left and didn't look at her again until she handed him a piece of paper, then he focused his attention on it.

"What's this?" he asked, staring at a list of names of people he'd never heard of before.

"A list of Shane Moore's closest friends and associates. His sister, Meagan, gave it to me."

Adam tried to ignore Isabel's nearness. The scent of her slightly spicy perfume wafted in the air, and he steeled himself against its evocative fragrance. "And what exactly do you intend to do with this?"

She moved back to her desk and sat on the edge. "Find out what they know. Surely somebody on that list knows where my father is being held, and who is responsible for his kidnapping. Shane Moore was only a pawn in somebody's bigger game, and I want that somebody." Her spring-colored eyes glittered in a way that Adam found distinctly disconcerting...he recognized the glitter as trouble.

When Isabel had served a tour of duty in the navy, Adam had been her commanding officer. He'd immediately found her to be highly intelligent and self-sufficient. He'd also found her headstrong, stubborn and unwilling to sit on the sidelines in lieu of taking action whenever possible.

He steadfastly refused to contemplate the other traits he found too attractive...such as the silky feel of her hair beneath his fingertips and the intimate press of her body against his.

He actively fought against the memory of the single moment when they'd both nearly forgotten themselves and their respective positions and had almost shared a forbidden kiss. Almost.

"And just what makes you think the people on this list will talk to you...confide in you?" he asked in an attempt to stay focused on business at hand, rather than pleasure never shared.

"I'm going to go undercover." She raised her chin and glared at him, as if challenging him to stop her.

"Need I remind your highness that it's only been a week since you were nearly shot in the back by Shane Moore?" What Adam would never tell her was how often in the last week he'd suffered nightmares about that moment when Shane's gun had been pointed at Isabel.

"If not for the quick action of your cousin, Luke, we wouldn't be having this conversation," he continued. "You wouldn't be talking with anyone."

She waved a hand, as if to dismiss the drama. "I'm still not convinced my dear cousin Luke doesn't have something to do with my father's disappearance."

"He saved your life," Adam observed.

She nodded, her eyes gleaming with the intelligence Adam had always admired. "He did, but at the same time did he also manage to kill a co-conspirator before he could talk?"

Adam sighed. "That thought has crossed my mind, too," he admitted. "But, you can't go undercover," he protested. "Your picture is in the paper all the time. People know who you are."

Adam tried not to think about the latest batch of pictures of her that had graced the society pages. In those photos she'd been dancing with a pretty-boy royal named Sebastian Lansbury, a distant cousin of the Thortons, the royal family from Roxbury, and a dandy if Adam had ever seen one.

The headlines had boldly announced the rumored engagement between the two and Adam had been surprised to feel a pang in his heart. That fair-haired fop in the pictures wasn't what a strong, independent, passionate woman like Isabel needed.

"People are used to seeing me looking like a princess," she replied and began to pace the small area in front of his chair.

Each time she swept past Adam, her fragrance tickled his nose and tantalized his senses. "Trust me, I can make it so nobody will ever recognize me as Princess Isabel."

"It's a foolish idea," Adam replied curtly.

"Why?" she shot back.

It was one of the things he'd always admired

about her, how she questioned authority, demanded rational explanations for decisions, and allowed herself to be open when those beneath her control did the same. It was also one of the things about her that irritated him.

She stopped her pacing and stood just in front of him, that familiar perfume enveloping him. "Tell me why you think it's foolish."

Because I don't want anything to happen to you. Because I can't imagine the world without you in it. Of course he didn't say these things, would never, ever say these things.

"You know what kind of a person Shane Moore was...he was dangerous, and I'd venture to guess that the people who were his associates, his friends and acquaintances are dangerous as well."

"Danger has never frightened me," she scoffed.

"And that's why you shouldn't do this," he returned evenly. "You know what your father would want...he'd want you here, working safely behind the scenes, not on the front lines risking your life."

He knew he'd irritated her, reminding her of the subject of much tension and debate between daughter and father. Her frown created a tiny wrinkle in the center of her forehead. "My father would want all of us to do whatever we can to find him. I'm tired of sitting and waiting around for somebody else to find him."

She began to pace once again, her shoulders stiff

with tension and her footsteps determined and purposeful. ''We know Shane Moore was responsible for my father's kidnapping. We know he was also responsible for kidnapping Ben.''

Lieutenant Ben Lockhart had agreed to impersonate King Michael's son, Nicholas, and had been kidnapped by Shane. Shane's sister, Meagan, had been responsible for Ben's safety and for the resulting unsuccessful attempted arrest of her brother...unsuccessful because Isabel's cousin, Luke, had shot and killed Shane.

''The key to who has my father and where they are keeping him is on that sheet of paper. I feel it...it's the only real lead we've had,'' she said fervently. ''Adam, Meagan already told us that she thinks my father had a stroke...for all we know he could be dying right now...all alone...in some horrid place.''

Her eyes grew too bright, and he realized she was on the verge of tears. He didn't want to see her cry. He'd only seen her cry once before, and at that time her tears had nearly undone him, nearly caused him to cross a line into forbidden territory.

He sighed with a sense of resignation. ''So, you're really intent on doing this?''

She nodded, a curt motion that sent the ends of her wavy hair to dancing on top of her shoulders. She drew a deep breath and, as if by magic, whatever emotion had momentarily possessed her was once again under control. "Since Meagan gave me this list, I've got Ben doing background checks on each name. I should have pictures and complete information about each of them by late this afternoon."

She was nothing if not efficient, he thought. He stood, unable to stay seated any longer. "I can't believe your cousin would be a party to this."

"Ben is a different man since he impersonated my brother and was kidnapped. He feels the same way I do...that if my father is still alive, time is running out and something has to be done. Besides, he knows I'm going to do this with or without his help." She raised her chin to him.

"I can't let you do this." He tried one last time to change her mind. "It's simply too dangerous. Give me all the information and I'll assign somebody to the job. I know a dozen men and women who would do anything to help find the king."

"No. I want to do this. Adam...I need to do this." There was a soft plea in her voice. "I've already made arrangements to rent a room above the King's Men Tavern. Meagan told me her brother and most of the names on this list spent a lot of time hanging out there."

The King's Men Tavern was near the palace, but few of the good king's men had ever been there. The place had a reputation for trouble, and far too often the police were called in to break up fights or arrest unruly drunks. He didn't like it. He didn't like it one bit.

But he could tell by looking at her that there was no point in trying to talk her out of it. Her features were taut, her chin raised in stubborn defiance. She intended to run with this…hook, line and sinker.

"And what is your back-up plan? One of the first things I ever taught you was that you never go into a dangerous situation without a back-up plan."

"You're my back-up plan," she said.

He eyed her in surprise.

She took a step closer to him, and again he could smell her perfume, that heady scent that made him think of hot summer nights and slick, silky skin.

He fought the impulse to back away from her, refusing to allow her to see any weakness on his part. "And what role am I going to play in this scheme of yours?" he asked.

"I'm going undercover as Bella Wilcox, Shane Moore's cousin." She reached into her pocket and withdrew something, then grabbed Adam's hand. "And you will be Adam Wilcox." She slid a plain gold band onto his ring finger. "My lawfully wedded husband."

Isabel sank into her chair and released a sigh as Adam left her office. She immediately buzzed her secretary. "Laura, please hold my calls and clear

my schedule for the rest of the afternoon and the
next two weeks.''

She heard her secretary's surprise, but the woman
was too professional to ask any questions. Too
wired to sit still, Isabel stood and began to pace the
small confines of her office.

If given a choice, she might have chosen somebody else to act as her "husband" in the undercover scheme. She and Adam had often butted
heads over military policies and procedures, but
that wasn't what bothered her about him.

What bothered her were his gunmetal gray eyes
with their sinfully long dark lashes. What bothered
her were his impossibly broad shoulders, his taut,
flat stomach and slender hips.

What bothered her was that when his gaze swept
over her, she forgot the trappings of her title and
the expertise of her training, and became simply a
woman with a woman's wants and needs.

There were times when Adam looked at her that
she felt her knees weaken and her stomach knot and
intense heat suffused her entire body. She knew it
would be wise to choose somebody else for this
undercover operation.

But for this particular assignment she needed the
best, and Adam was the best. Well-trained, with an
impressive record, Adam Sinclair was the only man
on earth she would trust with this important mission.

Adam Sinclair was also the only man on earth who had ever seen her cry. She frowned and tried to forget that there had been a time when she'd believed herself hopelessly in love with him. And that there had been a single moment in time when she'd practically thrown herself into his arms and he'd remained disappointingly professional.

She couldn't think about that now. That was in the past...in her youth. She had to focus on the task at hand. She knew her plan was dangerous, knew the people responsible for her father's kidnapping were dangerous. But she would do whatever it took to find her father and put an end to the chaos that reigned in the country she so loved.

Tonight she would put out the word that she was going into seclusion, that the stress of the past three months had finally caught up with her. And tomorrow night she would begin her charade as Bella Wilcox, cousin to Shane Moore and wife of Adam.

She shivered, unsure what had her more anxious, rubbing elbows with dangerous men and women or living a pretend marriage with Adam Sinclair.

Chapter Two

The interior of the King's Men Tavern was far worse than Adam had imagined. The moment he stepped inside, acrid cigarette smoke assaulted him, scratching the back of his throat and stinging his eyes.

The tension in the air was thick, hinting that an explosion of tempers and passions could be imminent.

From the back of the establishment, the dull whack of billiard balls could be heard, mixing with the clink of glasses and bottles and the raucous shouts of the players.

Adam spied an empty stool at the bar and made his way to it, conscious of the speculative gazes that followed his progress.

Although he didn't actively try to make eye contact with the tough guys in the place, he also didn't avoid it. He knew in a place like this any sign of weakness was an open invitation to confrontation. While he certainly wasn't afraid of anyone in the establishment, he also wasn't looking for trouble.

It was important for him and Isabel to maintain a low profile. He didn't want anyone looking too closely at him or her. Recognition could place them both in immediate danger.

He slid onto the stool, dropped his duffel bag to the floor and motioned to the bartender. The burly man approached wearing the world-weary expression of a man who would rather be anywhere than where he was.

Adam ordered a drink, then swiped a hand across his chin, unaccustomed to the scratchy whiskers along his jaw. In preparing for his role, he hadn't shaved since the day before. Instead of his usual pristine uniform, he was clad in a pair of tight jeans and a black T-shirt.

The bartender slammed his drink down and Adam picked it up and spun around on the stool so he could view the entire room.

Isabel should be arriving within the next fifteen minutes or so. Adam had arrived early so he could get a feel for the place. He'd never been in here before, although he'd heard many stories of the place.

He didn't like it. He didn't like it at all. The whole place stank of simmering violence and pathetic lies. He'd bet half the men in the room were felons, and the women didn't look much better. His attention was captured by one particular woman across the room.

She was a burst of flash and color in a room of blacks and grays. Her teased hair was the color of a shiny new penny and her gold sparkly midriff blouse clung to pert, rounded breasts and exposed a flat, well-toned abdomen.

Her short black skirt barely covered her other assets, and cupped her well-shaped bottom. If she bent over too far, there would be no mysteries left, Adam thought. But, he couldn't help but admire the sexy length of legs that disappeared into a pair of red spike high heels.

Obviously a working girl, he thought as he watched her chatting up a man who looked half drunk but managed to leer at her through bleary eyes.

Adam couldn't fault the man for leering. Although Adam couldn't discern the woman's facial features in the dimness of the room, if her face matched her shape, she was definitely one hot-looking ticket.

Watching the woman, Adam felt a surge of blood sweep through him and realized it had been some time since he'd been with a woman. Since his father's disappearance a little over a year before, Adam's life had been consumed with trying to clear his father's name...his own name. There had been no time and, truthfully, no inclination for romance.

Adam looked at his watch, then toward the front door. Just a few minutes after ten. Where in the hell was Isabel? They'd agreed to meet here at 10:00 p.m.

As soon as she walked in the door, he was going to grab her by the arm and steer her out of here. This was certainly no place for a princess. There had to be some other way to get the information Isabel sought.

He looked back at the woman across the room. Like a magnet, she drew him. As if she felt his gaze on her, she looked over to him. She grabbed the hand of the drunk standing next to her and began pulling him toward Adam.

Adam frowned, wondering if he'd committed some sort of faux pas merely by looking at the woman. Maybe the drunk was her pimp and they'd mistaken him for an interested john. He stood, unsure what to expect.

She drew close enough for him to see her features and he found himself admiring the full lips carefully colored with ruby-red lipstick, the high cheekbones pinkened with a blush of color and green eyes that suddenly caused shock to rivet through him.

He knew those green eyes. They weren't the eyes of a hooker...they were the eyes of a princess. It was Isabel.

Before he had time to assess the situation, before his shock had completely worn off, she launched herself into him, pressing her warm lithe body intimately against his.

"I was just telling Willie here about my handsome hunk of a husband, then I look across the room and there you are," she said, her head tilted back to look at him. "Now, kiss me, sweetheart, and show Willie just how glad you really are to see me."

Her eyes beseeched him to play the game and with his head still reeling from shock, with her body warm and soft against his and her perfume dizzying his senses, Adam could do nothing but comply.

Someplace in the back of his mind, as his mouth descended to hers, he knew this was a major mistake. She hadn't said anything about kissing her when she'd told him they were going undercover.

But, even knowing it was a mistake, Adam couldn't stop the maelstrom of excitement that coursed through him as he realized he was about to do what he'd dreamed of doing for years. He was going to kiss Princess Isabel Stanbury.

He'd intended the kiss to be a mere brushing of lips, a perfunctory touch of mouths. But, the moment his lips met hers, desire roared through him.

With the press of her breasts against his chest, and his fingers touching the silky warm bare skin of her lower back, Adam lost himself in the kiss.

Her mouth was hot and opened eagerly to him as her arms wound tight around his neck. She tasted sweeter, hotter than in any of his fantasies, and his senses reeled with the reality of her in his arms.

After what seemed like a sweet eternity and a disappointing nanosecond at the same time, she broke the kiss. She took a step back from him, her cheeks flushed a heated pink and her green eyes widened in shock.

"I'd say the man is definitely glad to see you," Willie snickered.

The man's words seemed to break the stunned spell that had momentarily gripped Isabel. "Adam, darling, this is Willie Tammerick. He was a friend of my cousin Shane. Willie, this is my husband, Adam Wilcox."

Adam nodded, disliking the way Willie's gaze slid over Isabel, as if she were a delectable treat that he couldn't wait to taste. He noticed other men in the bar looking at her in the same way.

He wanted to wrap his arms around her, find a coat and throw it over her, do whatever he could to hide the luscious curves she had on display. What was she thinking when she picked those revealing clothes? And what on earth had she done to her hair?

His blood boiled and he wasn't sure if it was because she'd been utterly shameless and irresponsible in choosing her clothes, or if it was a residual effect of the kiss they'd just shared.

Despite his reluctance, he draped a hand over Isabel's shoulder, keeping her close to his side and establishing a proprietorship to her for every other man in the bar.

"So, you were a friend of Shane's?" Adam asked, once again directing his attention to Willie Tammerick.

The man was a skinny weasel of a man, with eyes set slightly too close together, a long pointed nose and a scraggly gray beard that cried out for the touch of a sharp razor.

"Sure, Shane and me…we were like this." He held up two fingers twined together and stumbled slightly as if in raising his arm he'd thrown off his balance. "Poor Shane, shot to death by them royal guards like he was nothing but a damn dog."

Somehow Adam doubted that a man as smart as Shane Moore would have been close friends with Willie, who appeared to be nothing more than a loose-mouthed drunk.

"I guess Shane got into something over his head," Isabel said.

Willie grinned at her, a loopy smile that displayed a broken front tooth. "Now he's in way over his head…six feet under, he is." His smile fell away as he realized his morbid joke wasn't appreciated. "There's lots of us here that are going to miss old Shane. He was always good for buying a round or two."

He looked at Adam expectantly, obviously hoping Adam might spring for a round of drinks. Instead Adam focused his attention on a tall, burly man with tattoos decorating tree-trunk sized arms who was intently focused on Isabel.

Hunger. It radiated from the man's eyes and Adam found himself looking at Isabel not as a subordinate who had once served a tour of duty beneath him, not as a princess whom he was sworn to protect, but as a woman.

A woman with a killer body and a full, slightly pouty mouth that could muddy a man's thoughts. A woman who could cause a bar fight just by fluttering her blackened lashes.

As he watched, the man sauntered toward them. Adam tensed, anticipating possible trouble. He tightened his arm around Isabel, then breathed a sigh of relief as the man swept past them and toward the billiard tables in the back.

The last thing Adam wanted was a brawl. What he wanted was to get the scantily clad Isabel out of here before he had to fight for her honor.

"I need to talk to you," he said pointedly to Isabel.

Her eyes narrowed slightly and she nodded, then

flashed Willie a winsome smile. "We'll talk to you later, Willie. My old man wants to spend some time with me."

Her "old man?" Where on earth had the princess learned such slang? As Willie wandered away, Isabel took a key from the tiny glittery purse she carried.

"Our room is up on the third floor," she said and pointed to a doorway at the back of the bar. Beyond the doorway Adam could see a narrow staircase. "I haven't been up there yet. Just let me get my bag."

She stepped away from Adam and motioned to the bartender. "Bart, sweetie, can I have my bag?"

"Sure thing, doll." The stoic bartender beamed a smile and winked at her then grabbed a hot-pink duffel bag from someplace behind the bar and slung it onto the polished surface where Isabel could grab it.

Adam watched the flirtatious exchange between the two and felt as if he'd entered some alternate universe. From the moment he'd walked through the door, he'd felt off-center and fought against a growing sense of unease.

No, that wasn't exactly true. It hadn't been from the moment he'd walked through the door. It had been from the moment he'd seen her in that sexy get-up, and kissing her had only sent his senses further afield.

He felt utterly out of control and he didn't like it one little bit. It was definitely time to get some control back. As he followed Isabel up the steep staircase that led to the rented rooms above the bar, he tried not to notice how tight her skirt fit across her shapely bottom. He tried not to notice the wiggle that accompanied each of her steps.

And he desperately tried to ignore the shaft of heat that each wiggle shot through him. He couldn't do this. And she shouldn't do this.

This place was too dangerous, and her choice of clothing, the role she'd chosen to play, were like tossing a lit match into a can of kerosene.

And at the moment, he felt like that explosive can of kerosene.

Isabel was acutely conscious of Adam just behind her as she climbed the steep wooden stairs to the third floor. The moment she'd first seen him sitting on the stool at the bar, her breath had caught in her chest. In all the years she'd known Adam, worked with him, she'd never seen him out of uniform.

Clad in a tight pair of worn black jeans and a black T-shirt that hugged the hard, well-defined muscles of his torso, he had looked as dangerous, as on the edge as any man in the room. The scruffy growth of whiskers that darkened his jawline only added to his dangerous appeal.

And that kiss. Heat swept through her as she thought of that moment when Adam's lips had claimed hers. How many times had she fantasized about kissing him? Her fantasies hadn't even begun to live up to the real thing.

Nothing she'd experienced so far in her life had prepared her for the utter pleasure and intense excitement of Adam's kiss. In that single kiss, he'd claimed more than her lips, he'd stolen her breath and touched her frantically beating heart.

Adam didn't say a word as they made their way up, but she felt an angry tension rolling off him. She'd worked with Adam often enough in the past to recognize when he was angry. But, this time she wasn't sure what was causing his anger. So far their undercover subterfuge seemed to be working just fine.

By the time they reached the third floor she was slightly out of breath. She didn't know if it was from the physical exertion of climbing the stairs or her mind playing and replaying that kiss over and over again in her head.

She found their room and inserted the key into the lock. When she shoved open the door, she couldn't help but release a sigh of dismay. The place was a dump.

They stepped inside, and Adam closed the door behind them. "What did you expect? The Ritz?" he asked. His voice was curt, clipped.

"At least it looks relatively clean," she replied. It was true, the room was small, holding only a double bed, a cigarette-scarred nightstand and a lumpy chair. The only light in the room was an ugly lamp with a shade that sat askew. But, the carpet was clean and the room held the scent of a pine cleanser.

She peeked into the tiny bathroom. No tub, just a miniscule shower stall, but this room also looked clean. She turned and looked at Adam, who stood in the center of the room with a frown marring his handsome face. "It's not so bad," she said. "It could be worse."

"No, it's not so bad," he agreed, but she wasn't fooled by his affable reply. "And it doesn't really matter if it's bad or not because we are not going to stay here," he added.

Isabel looked at him in astonishment. "What are you talking about? Of course we're going to stay here. It's part of the plan."

"It's a ridiculous plan, and what have you done to your hair?" He looked at her as if she were an alien from another planet.

She reached up and touched a strand of her bright copper hair. "It's a rinse. The directions said it would wash out in a couple of weeks. It's part of my disguise."

"And what about those clothes? Where on earth did you get them?" His gray eyes glittered like hot metal in the sunshine. "You look like...you look like..."

"I look nothing like a princess," she interrupted. "And that was the whole idea." She frowned. She'd been so pleased at her selections, certain that her clothes would allow her to fit right into the crowd in the bar.

"Half the men in the room were ready to make a move on you," he exclaimed, his eyes stormy seas of anger.

She shrugged, surprised yet oddly pleased by this piece of information. "Really? But that's good then. It means my disguise worked."

He eyed her ruefully. "Isabel, they probably thought you were a working woman and wondered what kind of fee you charged."

"You mean they thought I was...I am...a hooker?" she squeaked and sank down on the edge of the bed. "Maybe I did overdo it a bit," she admitted ruefully and looked down at her tiny skirt and midriff top. "But, at least it worked, nobody recognized me as a princess." She flashed a smile in hopes of breaking the tension.

He didn't return the smile, but rather began to pace in front of her. Clad all in black, he looked like a dangerous panther seeking an escape route.

Isabel waited for him to speak, knowing he wouldn't until he had his thoughts in order. It was one of the things that had always driven her crazy about him. Adam never did or said anything spontaneously.

He finally stopped pacing and stood before her. "I won't allow you to do this, Isabel."

She stood and narrowed her eyes, rebelling against the authoritative tone of his voice. "You won't allow me to do this?" she asked.

She stepped so close to him she could feel the heat radiating from his body, see the tiny silver flecks that gave his gray eyes a magnetic depth. "You forget, Adam. You aren't my commanding officer anymore. You can't stop me from doing this."

"That's true." His gaze focused on her lips and suddenly the thought of the kiss they had shared filled her mind.

Without her volition she licked her lips, her mouth unaccountably dry. "I intend to do this, Adam, with or without your help. Either you are with me or you are against me."

He took a step back from her and raked a hand through his short hair in obvious frustration. "You know I can't walk out and leave you alone in this place."

She nodded, a sense of relief flooding through her. "Then you're with me."

"You've given me very little choice," his voice was rich with irritation. "I'm with you on one condition," he said. His gaze didn't quite meet hers.

"You promise me you won't wear that outfit again. I don't want to have to battle the wise guys in this place for your honor."

"And you would do that? Fight for my honor?" she teased.

"Of course I would," he replied instantly. "It's my job to protect and serve the king and his family."

Isabel wasn't sure why, but his answer disappointed her. He never forgot his position as a commanding officer in the Royal Edenbourg Navy. Just once, she wished he would forget their respective positions, forget duty and responsibility and meet her simply as a man meeting a woman.

"Did you get some background information from Ben?" he asked.

She nodded and reached for her duffel bag. Clothing spilled out onto the bed as she dug in the bottom for the papers that contained material they would need in their attempt to connect with Shane Moore's associates.

She pulled out the papers, stuffed the clothes back into the bag, and then patted the space next to her for Adam to sit. He eased down next to her, bringing with him a scent of minty soap and spicy cologne. She held the papers out before her and he leaned into her to read them with her.

"This is the list of the names of people we now know were associates of Shane's," she said, trying to focus on the business at hand and ignore how warm his thigh was against hers despite the barrier of his jeans.

"We already made contact with Willie Tammerick. Here's the information Ben was able to pull up on him." She shuffled the papers, her fingers becoming all thumbs as Adam leaned even closer, his shoulder rubbing hers.

"No surprises there," he murmured. "The man has a history of arrests for drunk and disorderly, public nuisance and disturbing the peace."

His breath was warm on the side of her face and again she found herself remembering their kiss. His mouth had been so hot and had tasted of a hunger that had momentarily stolen her breath away.

No kiss in her entire life had affected her like Adam's, torching her deep in the pit of her stomach, touching her in a primal place that had never been touched before by any man.

"Isabel." The single word held a touch of exasperation and she realized he'd been talking to her, but she'd not been listening.

"I'm sorry, I got distracted. What did you say?"

"I said I can't imagine Shane Moore confiding anything important to Willie. Shane was too smart to confide in a drunk."

Isabel nodded. "I think you're probably right. I talked to Willie for a while before you came in tonight and tried to pump him for information, but

I don't think he has any idea what Shane was involved in.''

Ben Lockhart had done an excellent job in pulling together background material on most of the people on the list from Meagan Moore. Not only had he detailed their rap sheets, but also when possible, he'd obtained a photograph.

For the next two hours, Adam and Isabel pored over the information. Adam pointed to one of the pictures Ben had provided of a burly man with tattoos.

"Blake Hariman," Isabel said, reading the name beneath the photo. "Nice guy. His arrests include armed robbery, possession of a deadly weapon and aggravated assault.''

"And according to Ben's information, he was one of Shane's closest friends.'' Adam gazed at her intently. "Isabel, we're playing a dangerous game with dangerous people here. If any one of them get the faintest hint that we aren't what they think, what we're pretending, then we could wind up dead.'' His expression was somber, his eyes deep pools of gray mist.

"I know," she agreed. "But, there's no reason for anyone to suspect us of being anything other than Bella and Adam Wilcox. I told Bart, the bartender, that you're looking for work and he said he might be able to set you up doing odd jobs around here. I think we're pretty solid in our disguise, Adam.''

For the first time since they'd entered the room, Adam smiled. Isabel felt the power of his smile right down to her toes. Adam was an attractive man when he was somber, but when he smiled, he was absolutely devastating.

''We sure don't have to worry about anyone recognizing you. I've never known a bottle of rinse and some makeup to make such a difference. I watched you for several minutes before I finally realized that you were you.''

''You were watching me?'' Isabel eyed him curiously, a sweeping warmth shooting through her. Had he been watching her because he'd thought she looked good?

His smile fell from his features, and was replaced by a frown. ''I was watching everyone,'' he replied. He got up from the bed and looked at his watch. ''It's after midnight. Shouldn't we call it a night?''

Isabel nodded and quickly gathered up the papers and shoved them back into her duffel bag. She stood and was suddenly struck by just what ''call it a night'' would entail.

She and Adam were pretending to be man and wife. They would spend the night in this room together. Tonight, and every night for as long as they played this game, they would sleep side by side in the bed that suddenly looked far too small.

Chapter Three

"Traitor!" The crowd of people shouted, their fists raised in rage. "You're a traitor to the crown!" The mood was wicked...dangerous and several of the people picked up rocks and threw them at the man before them.

The man, resplendent in a naval uniform with ribbons and medals decorating his chest, didn't flinch, didn't attempt to escape the crowd's wrath.

Adam watched in horror as his father was stoned. Then suddenly the scene changed and it was Adam being stoned. The rocks of various sizes and shapes thudded painfully into his body as the crowd feverishly chanted.

"Traitor!"

"Traitor!"

There was no hazy transition from sleep to awareness. One minute he was dreaming and the next moment he was wide awake, the horrid nightmare merely a bitter aftertaste in his mouth.

He was instantly aware of aching bones and sore muscles, but knew the soreness wasn't from a nightmare stoning, but rather from attempting to sleep in the lumpy chair next to the bed.

He pulled himself upright from his slumped position and checked the luminous dial of his wristwatch. Almost two. Despite the lateness of the hour, light illuminated the spaces around the curtains at the window. Adam knew the light came from the bright sign that proclaimed the name of this establishment.

He focused his gaze on the bed, where Isabel slept soundly. She was on her back and the sheet had fallen down around her waist, giving him a tantalizing view of her rounded breasts covered with the thin lilac silk of her nightgown.

He knew he shouldn't look, but he couldn't help but drink in the lovely sight of her. In sleep her features took on a soft vulnerability rarely seen when she was awake. Her long lashes cast shadows beneath her eyes and her mouth was opened slightly, as if awaiting a lover's kiss. Her skin looked creamy and touchable.

Frowning, he jerked his gaze away from her.

It had been awkward when they'd prepared to go

to bed. Adam hadn't contemplated all that this subterfuge would entail. He'd certainly not considered the fact that it might include sleeping with Isabel.

He'd changed from his clothing into a pair of athletic shorts in the bathroom while she'd gotten into her nightgown in the bedroom. Then, once she'd gotten into bed, Adam had left the bathroom and insisted he would spend the night on the chair.

Pulling himself up, he silently walked the length of the room in an effort to unkink muscles, and tried to keep his gaze away from the slumbering princess. But it was impossible.

It was as if in sleep she called to him and he found himself at the edge of the bed, gazing at her more openly, more intently than he ever did when she was awake.

From the first moment he'd laid eyes on her, he'd found her beautiful, with an earthy edge to her features that whispered of a latent sexuality.

He frowned once again, pulled his gaze away from her and instead stepped over to the window. Pulling the curtain aside, he peered outside and to the deserted street below. But his thoughts were distant.

Thinking of the nightmare he'd suffered, his stomach clenched tight and he felt the suffocating press of emotion inside his chest. For a little over a year he'd lived in the shadow of the suspicions about his father.

He knew his father wasn't a traitor, would never sell out to another country, but knowing and proving were two different things. He'd been trying to find out exactly what had happened to Admiral Jonathon Sinclair when Isabel had called him home because of the kidnapping of King Michael.

And so, his personal mission had been put on hold for a greater mission…to find Isabel's kidnapped father. He let the curtain fall closed once again, then turned as he heard Isabel stir.

She turned her head and opened her eyes, appearing drowsy and still half-asleep. "Adam?"

"I'm right here," he replied softly.

"What are you doing?"

"Just prowling a bit. I couldn't sleep."

She stretched languidly. "That's because you're trying to sleep in that awful chair. Come to bed, Adam. Nothing terrible will happen if we share the bed." Almost before the words were out of her mouth, her eyes had drifted closed and she was once again asleep.

Adam contemplated her words. *Nothing terrible will happen if we share the bed.* He didn't want to think about getting back on that chair, with its lumpy back and ill-stuffed seat.

But, the vision of Isabel in that gold short top and that miniscule skirt haunted him. As they'd discussed the various people on Meagan Moore's list, Isabel's full, ruby lips had taunted him, and her floral-and-spice scent had made concentration difficult.

He was accustomed to seeing her in a business setting, with both of them in uniform, not in a casual setting with her wearing next to nothing.

With a tired sigh, he threw himself back into the torturous chair. She might not think anything terrible would happen if they shared the bed, but he wasn't so sure. In his state of heightened awareness where she was concerned, he wasn't sure he could trust himself.

When he awakened again, dawn was trying to seep in around the edges of the curtain. With a groan, Adam struggled to his feet, his back an aching mass of muscle from the awkward position of his sleep.

Isabel was still asleep. She'd claimed the very center of the bed and was sprawled on her stomach, her face buried in one of the pillows.

Although it was early, Adam knew he couldn't sleep anymore. He rarely required more than three or four hours anyway. Quietly, he pulled clean clothes from his duffel bag, then went into the bathroom.

A moment later, standing beneath a surprisingly hot, strong spray of water in the shower, Adam thought about the task ahead of him and Isabel.

He knew the investigation into the king's kidnapping had begun with the focus on the immediate family members and their friends. Nobody had been spared scrutiny, including King Michael's brother, Edward, who had now assumed the king's responsibilities, and his two sons, Luke and Blake. Since Michael's kidnapping, Blake had married Rowena Wilde, Isabel's lady-in-waiting.

No red flags had gone up with anyone who had been investigated so far, leaving everyone to speculate on just who had been giving Shane Moore his orders. Who had been responsible for the king's kidnapping? And why?

In a last-ditch effort to force the hand of the conspirators, a rumor had been circulated that Prince Nicholas had been found dead, but so far that rumor had prompted no move from the guilty.

Today was Shane Moore's funeral and Adam wondered how many of Shane's cohorts would show up to pay their respects. Although Isabel hadn't mentioned it yet, he had a feeling he and "Bella Wilcox" would be among the bereaved.

He sighed and shut off the shower. He hoped he and Isabel weren't in over their heads. He knew if anything happened to Isabel while she was with him, it would be another nail in the coffin of his family name.

Dressing, he shoved these thoughts out of his head. He couldn't focus on his family problem now. He had to stay focused on pretending to be Adam Wilcox, not Lieutenant Commander Adam Sinclair.

He stepped out of the bathroom, surprised to see Isabel awake and propped up on the pillows. The sheet demurely covered her, only a whisper of lilac silk visible at her shoulders.

"I hope you saved me some hot water," she said, a little edge of crankiness in her voice.

"And good morning to you, too," Adam said dryly.

She frowned and raked a hand through her hair. "I don't suppose this place has room service."

"Ha, fat chance," Adam retorted. He sat on the chair to put on his shoes. "But, if you'll get dressed, we should be able to find a place to have breakfast someplace nearby."

"Coffee...that's what I need," she said as she shoved the covers back and stood.

Adam averted his gaze, but not before he caught a glimpse of her with the silky nightgown clinging to every curve. His internal temperature skyrocketed, and he was grateful when she disappeared into the bathroom.

He scrubbed a hand down his face and leaned back in the chair. This was going to be harder than he'd thought. He hadn't slept well and was already dreading another night on the damnable chair.

However, the thought of lying next to Isabel on the too-soft mattress, the thought of feeling her body heat washing over him, filled him with an almost unbearable tension.

He'd fought his feelings for Isabel for years. First, when she'd been a recruit under his command. Even then, there had been awareness between the two of them, a heady tension that had filled him both with excitement and dread.

Any relationship between an officer and a recruit was strictly forbidden, and neither of them had been willing to jeopardize their careers for a tempestuous foray into romance, no matter how appealing that romance might have been.

But, you aren't her commanding officer anymore, a small voice whispered inside his head. True, he wasn't. But, she was a princess, and he was a man with a dishonorable stain on his family name.

Half the people in the country of Edenbourg believed his father was a traitor. Adam certainly wasn't a potential suitor for Princess Isabel.

Besides, if the newspapers were correct, she was already bound to the pretty-boy Sebastian Lansbury and King Michael had given his approval to the match right before his kidnapping.

It was best for Adam to keep his mind on two goals…the first was to find the king, and the second was to clear his father's name. Isabel was just as taboo for him now as when she'd been his recruit and he'd been her commanding officer. And he would do well to remember that over the next couple of weeks.

* * *

Isabel polished off the last of her second buttered croissant, feeling much better than she had when she'd first awakened.

She and Adam sat in a small café just down the street from the King's Men Tavern. It was early enough in the morning that only a few patrons drifted in as Adam and Isabel ate breakfast.

Isabel was once again clad in "Bella" clothes, although she'd chosen the least risqué of what she'd packed in deference to Adam's wishes.

Bright purple slacks hugged her tightly, and a blouse the same hue clashed cheerfully with her hair color. Spike heels and dangly earrings completed her fashion statement for the day.

Adam was a lot less creative in his dress code. He was clad in another pair of black jeans and a clean gray T-shirt that did magnificent things to his gray eyes.

"That was the best croissant and coffee I've had in months," she said.

"It certainly seems to have improved your mood," he observed dryly.

She grinned, unable to protest his words. "I'm not much of a morning person. I don't function very cheerfully until I've had a morning cup of coffee."

"I gathered that." He motioned to the waitress for a refill of their coffee cups.

"Shane's funeral is at ten," she said when the

waitress had departed from their table. "We'll take a taxi to the cemetery."

"Are you sure it's wise we go?" he asked. "Surely some of the royal investigators will be there. We don't want to be recognized."

She smiled and eyed him objectively. "I don't think we have to worry about being recognized. I don't look like me, and with all those whiskers you've sprouted, you don't look like you."

What she couldn't tell him was that she'd always found him exceedingly handsome, but with the dark shadows of whiskers on his cheeks and in the casual clothing that emphasized his muscular fitness, he nearly stole her breath away.

"It's important that we see who shows up at the funeral, Adam. The mastermind of the whole kidnapping scheme might be there," she said, trying to stay focused.

"I doubt it," Adam replied and took a sip of his coffee. "Whoever is behind the scheme is far too smart to show up and publicly announce his ties to a fallen comrade."

Isabel sighed in discouragement. "You're probably right. I just wish...I just desperately want to be the one to find Father."

"Isabel." Adam reached across the small table and placed his hand on hers. "You don't have to prove yourself to anyone, especially not to your father."

Isabel frowned, finding his words surprising and his touch more than a little bit disturbing. She pulled her hand away. "You don't know anything about my relationship with my father," she protested. "And you better start practicing calling me Bella, not Isabel."

"I know how upset you were when he refused to allow you to continue your tour of duty with the navy."

"That was a long time ago," she replied, not quite meeting his gaze. "I realize Father was only making the decision he thought best for me."

Although it was what she'd told herself over and over again, the pain of her father's decision was still with her. She'd loved being in the military and it was the night her father had told her she couldn't extend her tour of duty that she'd wept in Adam's arms.

As he'd held her on that night, attempting to console her, she'd realized she wasn't sure if she'd wanted to remain in the navy for her career, or simply to continue being near Adam.

It hadn't mattered anyway, for on that night she'd raised her lips to him, and he'd turned away, telling her without actually saying the words that there was no future between them, that he had no personal feelings toward her.

"You would have made a terrific intelligence officer," Adam said softly.

A burst of warmth swept through her at his words. "Thank you," she said simply. But she cradled the words to her heart, knowing Adam wasn't given to false compliments or platitudes.

They lingered over their breakfast, as if reluctant to return to their cramped living space. As they drank more coffee, they spoke of inconsequential things...movies they'd seen, favorite music, people they both knew.

There were moments when Adam's eyes grew dark, deep with thought, and she wondered if he was thinking about his father. She hadn't told him that when she'd called him home to help find the king, she'd assigned a task force of two of Edenbourg's best investigators to dig deep into the disappearance of Adam's father.

Like Adam, she couldn't believe the highly decorated retired Admiral Jonathon Sinclair had sold out and disappeared from Edenbourg along with a fighter plane prototype worth billions of dollars and priceless in high-tech applications.

At nine-thirty, they left the café and grabbed a taxi to take them to the cemetery where Shane Moore would be laid to rest. They asked the driver to wait there until they were ready to leave.

At the cemetery, they found a dismally small group of people gathered around the casket bearing the dead rebel. They joined the group and Isabel scanned the faces of the people, identifying several from the pictures Ben had gathered.

Willie Tammerick, already looking three sheets to the wind, nodded to the two of them as the minister began to intone a passionless eulogy that made it obvious he had not known Shane personally.

Conspicuously absent was Meagan, Shane's sister. When Lieutenant Ben Lockhart had impersonated Prince Nicholas and gotten himself kidnapped by Shane, it had been Meagan who had come to Ben's defense, and ultimately the two had fallen in love.

Isabel shot a surreptitious glance at Adam. In all the years she had known him, in all the time they had worked closely together, she had no idea if he'd ever been in love. She didn't even know if he believed in love.

But, there had been a time when she'd believed herself in love with him, a time when she'd believed the sun rose and set on Adam Sinclair. She told herself she'd outgrown those feelings, but that didn't explain why he still made her heart race just a little faster than normal, why when he directed those gorgeous gray eyes at her, she felt both hot and cold at the same time.

Frowning, she once again scanned the funeralgoers, her gaze falling on a woman who stood at the edge of the small group.

She was a tall, buxom blonde and would have

been quite pretty if not for the tears that raced down her face, reddening her nose and swelling her eyes.

A jolt of adrenaline swept through Isabel. Pam Sommersby. It had to be her. She'd seen mention of the woman in the notes from Ben, but there had been no photograph of Shane Moore's girlfriend, instead there had only been a physical description.

Isabel grabbed Adam's arm and squeezed until he looked down at her questioningly. She gestured toward the woman with a nod of her head. Adam followed her gesture, then looked back at Isabel. She reached up on her tiptoes so she could whisper in his ear. "I think that's Shane's girlfriend, Pam Sommersby."

Adam leaned down to whisper his reply in her ear. "We'll try to talk to her after the service."

Isabel nodded, distracted by his warm breath in her ear, the scent of his cologne that seemed to envelop her in a spicy cocoon.

She focused once again on the minister, who was finishing up with a prayer. When the service was over, the small group of people dispersed quickly, leaving only the black-clad sobbing blonde.

Isabel and Adam returned to their cab, but stood by the doors, waiting to approach the grieving woman. Isabel wanted to hate the woman who had been the girlfriend of the man responsible for her father's kidnapping. But, as she watched the woman place a single rose on Shane Moore's casket, saw the absolute agony of her heartbreak, Isabel couldn't help but feel a touch of pathos for her.

It wasn't until the woman left the gravesite and started walking toward a dark sedan that Isabel hurried after her.

"Pam," Isabel called. "Pam Sommersby."

The woman stopped and looked back over her shoulder. Her eyes widened and her mouth fell open in surprise. She turned and quickened her footsteps.

"Pam, stop! I just want to talk to you."

Before Isabel could reach her, Pam yanked open the car door and hopped inside. She started the car, gunned the engine, and then took off in a swirl of dust down the lane that led out of the cemetery.

Isabel turned and raced back to Adam, who was already in the cab and waiting. She dove into the back seat as Adam directed the cabbie to follow Pam's car.

"We can't let her get away," Isabel exclaimed as she leaned forward over the seat. She knew that in the material Ben had gathered there was no known address for Pam Sommersby.

"She knows something. I know she does." Isabel grabbed Adam's hand and squeezed tightly as the cab careened around a corner in pursuit of Pam's sedan.

"We'll get her," Adam said confidently. "We're gaining on her."

Isabel continued to hold Adam's hand as suddenly her emotions were racing as fast as the two speeding vehicles.

For three long months she'd been strong. For three long months she'd eagerly awaited a break...a clue that would lead to her missing father.

The news that her father might possibly have suffered a stroke while in captivity had filled her with a fear she'd suppressed until this very moment.

Now that fear battled with the hope that Pam Sommersby had the information they needed to save Isabel's father. She might be the only link they had to gain that information.

Traffic grew more dense and it was obvious Pam was no stranger to evasive driving tactics. She wove in and out of the traffic and each time her car disappeared from view a horrifying panic pressed in on Isabel's chest.

Pam had the answers. Isabel knew in her heart that Pam was the key to finding the king. They couldn't let her escape them. They just couldn't!

"She's going toward the King's Men Tavern," Adam exclaimed.

True to Adam's words, she turned down the alley just behind the tavern, and by the time the cab made the corner, Pam Sommersby's car was nowhere in sight.

"I don't see her," the cabbie said as he eased off the gas pedal.

"Keep driving," Isabel cried. "Go slow...she has to be here somewhere."

They crept down the alley, looking in the spaces between buildings, in open garages that they passed, but without success. It was as if the ground had opened up and swallowed Pam's car.

"Bella...we lost her," Adam finally said softly as the cab driver pulled to a halt.

Isabel stumbled from the car, vaguely aware of Adam paying the cabbie.

All the emotions she'd stuffed deep inside her the past three months bubbled to the surface. As the cab pulled away, Isabel's inner strength ebbed and tears blurred her vision.

It was as if any hope she might have entertained that they'd find her father had vanished with the cab. She looked up at Adam, as if in him she could rediscover hope, could again find her strength.

An uncontrollable sob escaped her as Adam wrapped her in his big strong arms and pulled her against his chest. Silently, he gave her permission to be weak, and for just this moment she needed to be weak.

She buried her face in the clean-smelling front of his shirt and released the tears of frustration and fear.

Chapter Four

Almost instantly Adam knew Isabel's tears were about more than the fact that they'd lost Pam Sommersby. He'd watched her for the past two months, worked with her in an effort to locate the missing king, and he'd marveled at her objectivity, the very strength of purpose that possessed her.

However, through the past two months Adam hadn't forgotten that the man they sought was not only the king of their country, but Isabel's father as well. And Adam knew all about the ache, the depth of pain that could eat at the soul when a father went missing.

Her tears seemed to come from the very depths of her and he was helpless to do anything but hold her until the storm of emotions passed.

Initially, he tried to focus on their surroundings. The alley was narrow and smelled of garbage. His gaze scanned the many buildings and garages and he knew that one of the buildings, one of those garages now housed Pam Sommersby's car.

If somebody had told him that the day would come when he would be standing in a stinking alley behind a rough-and-tumble tavern holding a sobbing Princess Isabel, he would have thought they were hallucinating.

And as much as he'd like to keep his focus on the alley, it was difficult to focus on anything other than Isabel in his arms. She fit so neatly against him, and her body was like a stick of fire radiating an evocative heat.

Her hair smelled clean, with a subtle scent of vanilla. As he held her, smelling the sweet fragrance of her, feeling the warmth of her body pressed so close, his mind filled with the memory of another time when he'd held her while she'd cried.

At that time he'd been her commanding officer and she'd come to him heartbroken because her father had forbidden her to pursue a military career.

Adam had held her while she'd wept and had found himself fighting an overwhelming desire for her. It was a desire that had built during their months of working together, a desire he knew could destroy his career.

He felt the same desire now. It was a need that formed a ball of heat in the pit of his stomach, and that heat radiated outward, traveling the entire length of his body.

You aren't her commanding officer anymore, a small voice whispered inside his head. There is no reason you can't follow through on your desire, no reason to ignore the fact that you want her.

As that tiny internal voice bewitched him with sweet possibilities, Isabel raised her head and looked up at him. In the depths of her luminous green eyes and the slight tremble of her lower lip, again he thought of the last time he'd held her like this.

That time she'd looked at him beseechingly, her lips parted to invite a kiss. Despite the desire that had roared through him, Adam had done the right thing. He'd dropped his hands from around her and had gently pushed her away.

Now as she gazed at him and the internal voice reminded him that there would be no repercussions to his career or hers, without conscious thought, Adam claimed her mouth with his.

He took her mouth in hunger and she responded in kind, opening her mouth and encouraging his tongue to deepen the kiss. And he did, swirling and dancing his tongue with hers.

Her hands grasped at his shoulders, as if in an attempt to get closer. It was as if she didn't just want to be next to him, but wanted to meld into him, become a part of him.

Adam fell into the kiss, losing all concept of place and time, all sense of identity. He was no longer Lieutenant Commander Adam Sinclair. He was Adam Wilcox, kissing his wife, Bella. He was simply a man kissing the woman he desired more than any other woman on earth.

His hands stroked up her back and he could feel the press of her breasts intimately against his chest. His desire for her electrified him.

He wanted to strip away the clothes that were at the moment an irritating barrier, he wanted to stroke every inch of her skin until they were both gasping in exquisite pleasure.

A horn blared from someplace nearby, yanking Adam back to reality. Reality was they were standing in the middle of a stinking alley. He was not really Adam Wilcox and the woman he was kissing was not his Bella.

She was Princess Isabel and unofficially betrothed to Sebastian Lansbury. And he was Lieutenant Commander Adam Sinclair, the only son of a man who was suspected of being a traitor to the crown.

"Come on, let's get out of here." Adam took Isabel by the arm. Silently they left the alley and returned to the King's Men Tavern.

They didn't speak until they were back in their third-floor room.

"Adam, I'm sorry," she said as soon as he closed the door.

"Sorry?" He eyed her intently, wondering what, exactly, she was apologizing for. For kissing him so deeply, so sweetly that he'd momentarily forgotten all the reasons he shouldn't have her...couldn't have her?

"I apologize for losing control like that." She sat on the edge of the bed, still looking achingly vulnerable. "Normally, I don't let my emotions get the better of me"

"There's nothing to apologize for," he replied briskly. He sat in the lumpy chair that had served as his bed the night before. He was irritated with himself, for momentarily losing control.

Isabel raked a hand through her copper-colored hair. "You can't imagine what the past months have been like...not knowing if my father is dead or alive." The instant the words left her mouth, her eyes widened. "But, of course you can imagine...your father..." She leaned forward, her eyes sparkling emeralds. "Tell me about him, Adam. Tell me about your father."

Pain usurped his irritation and shot through Adam like a hot poker at the mention of his father. It was a pain he'd lived with for the past year, a pain that seemed to have become as much a part of him as his gray eyes or his dark hair.

In all the time that Adam and Isabel had worked together since the fateful day of his father's disappearance, neither of them had ever mentioned it aloud. In truth, Adam had talked about it with nobody.

Adam had never discussed the uncertainty, the confusion, and the utter pain of his tumultuous emotions where his father was concerned.

"What do you want to know about him?" he finally asked.

"I don't know...anything. Were the two of you close? Was he a good father?"

Adam had the feeling she needed to hear him talk about his father so she wouldn't think about her own. He nodded. "We were very close. My mother died when I was eight, so there were just the two of us and Mrs. Gentry, our housekeeper."

"It must have been difficult, with your father being career military."

"Not really. Wherever dad was stationed, Mrs. Gentry and I followed." A warmth seeped through him as he thought of those years with his father. They had traveled to various bases, sometimes for mere months, other times for years, but Adam's memories of those times were all good.

"It was my father who instilled in me a love for the navy. However, much to his chagrin, I didn't follow in his footsteps and become a navy pilot. My father loves to fly, but I prefer to have both feet planted firmly on the ground.''

"But he was pleased when you decided to join the navy?'' she asked.

Adam leaned back in the chair, a smile curving his lips. "He told me that the day I enlisted was the happiest day of his life.'' The smile faded and he frowned thoughtfully. "And I think the saddest day of his life was the day he had to retire. The navy had been his wife, his lover…his very life, and without it he was positively lost.''

In truth, Jonathon Sinclair had become extremely depressed upon his retirement. And it was the memory of that deep depression that had haunted Adam when the talk of treason had first reared its ugly head.

In his gut, in the very depth of his heart, Adam knew his father would never, could never do anything against the country he loved, the country he'd sworn to protect and serve.

But there were times in the very dark of night when doubts whispered across his mind. Had Jonathon's depression also brought with it an anger against the country that had used him up then put him out to pasture?

"Dad was thrilled when they asked him to be a part of the Phantom team. The project gave him new life, a reason to get up in the mornings.''

Adam knew he was talking too much, exposing pieces of himself that he would not be able to retrieve. But, Isabel's gaze compelled him to continue and he felt as if a dam had broken inside him and the words and emotions had to gush out.

He leaned forward once again. "He was so excited about the project. He pored over blueprints day and night, huddled with top scientists and technicians, determined to make the Phantom the best fighter plane ever known."

"So, what happened, Adam?" Isabel got up off the bed and knelt by the side of his chair. "Your father and two pilots took the Phantom for a test flight, and the plane, your father and those two pilots disappeared. No wreckage was ever found."

"I know." The words whispered from him painfully. And because no wreckage had been found, speculation was that Admiral Jonathon Sinclair and the two pilots had sold out to foreign interests.

Rumor had it that the billion-dollar state-of-the-art plane was now hidden away on foreign soil and that the three men who had been in the plane were now sitting on some sunny beach enjoying millions of dollars...the price paid for treason.

But, Adam knew the real price of treason was a pain that broke the heart and a shame that seared the soul.

"I really don't know what happened," Adam said. His heart ached with a torturous depth of pain.

His father had always been his hero, and Adam wasn't sure which was worse—believing him gone forever, or believing him a traitor. "But, I'll tell you this...there are really only two possibilities. Either my father is alive and a traitor, or he's dead."

He was surprised by the thick emotion in his voice. He cleared his throat, uncomfortable to realize how close he was to losing it...closer than he could remember being for a very long time. He forced a smile. "I hope you'll get a happier ending when we find your father."

"Oh, Adam. I'm so sorry." Her eyes shone with a deep empathy. Before he could guess her intent, she stood, then sat on his lap. With a deep sigh she wrapped her arms tightly around his neck.

She laid her head against his shoulder and held on to him with a fierceness that surprised him. It was as if she believed if she held him tight enough, she could keep him from falling into the black abyss of his emotions.

And to his surprise...it worked.

Twenty-four hours before, Isabel never would have crawled onto Adam's lap to offer him comfort. But now she felt as if she were merely reciprocating the tenderness and caring he had shown her when they'd first gotten out of the cab.

For the past two months he'd been doing everything he could to help her find her missing father, to support her through the ordeal. And all the while he'd been burdened by the heartache of his own father's disappearance.

She wanted to tell him that she'd assigned a couple of investigators to continue to delve into the mystery of the vanished plane and the men aboard, but she was afraid of giving him false hope. It was possible Adam would never have any answers. She tightened her grip around his neck.

"Isabel." His voice was soft, and she felt his heartbeat thudding a pace that seemed too frantic to be normal.

"Yes?" she replied without moving.

"We should probably get down to the bar, see what information we can gather." He didn't move either and she wondered if he liked holding her as much as she liked being held by him.

"Isabel." This time his voice held a distinct edge of irritation. He stood without warning, forcing her to her feet. His features were taut, his eyes expressionless chunks of granite. "We need to get back to work."

Heat flushed her neck and face, the heat of humiliation. "Of course," she said briskly. "Let's get back to work."

A few moments later she followed Adam down the stairs to the tavern, a lingering embarrassment sweeping through her. What was wrong with her?

What had she been thinking? To curl up in his arms and hug him with such abandon.

The answer was that she hadn't been thinking at all. Since the moment in the cemetery when she'd recognized Pam Sommersby among the mourners, Isabel had been functioning on sheer emotion, which was not only uncharacteristic, but also foolish.

Just because Adam Sinclair was handsome as sin and had beautiful, sexy eyes that melted her insides, just because they were playing house at the moment and shared a common concern for their missing fathers, didn't mean there was anything personal between them.

She would not make the mistake again of trying to make it personal. This was about finding her father, and Adam had given absolutely no indication that he intended it to be anything more.

She'd obviously irritated him with her demonstration of compassion. She certainly wouldn't make that mistake again.

The minute she and Adam sat down at a table near the front door of the tavern, Will Tammerick joined them. Adam ordered the three of them a drink, earning a grin of approval from Willie.

"It was rather a sad turnout for Shane," Isabel observed once they had been served.

"Yeah, most of Shane's friends suddenly don't want to be associated with him, at least not in public. Nobody wants royal security breathing down their necks." Willie downed his drink in two thirsty gulps. Adam signaled for another.

"And you aren't afraid of royal security breathing down your neck?" Isabel asked him.

Willie laughed. "I got nothing to hide. Me and Shane, we were drinking buddies, but I sure as hell didn't know he was in on kidnapping the king. He must have got sucked in with that group of weirdos he started running with."

Adam and Isabel exchanged a quick glance. "Group of weirdos?" Adam echoed.

"Yeah, rebel types that call themselves the Patriots, or some such nonsense." Willie snorted derisively. "What they are is a bunch of miserable misfits who all hate the Stanburys."

Isabel knew there were people in Edenbourg who wanted to destroy the monarchy, but she'd never heard of a group called the Patriots before. She made a mental note to have Ben do some research on the group.

"Who doesn't hate the Stanburys?" Adam replied, an odd fervent light in his eyes. "They're the haves and we're the have nots in this country. It's too bad somebody doesn't kidnap all of them, every damn Stanbury on earth." Adam slammed his fist down on the table, as if to punctuate his sentence.

Both Isabel and Willie jumped at the punctuation.

"I'm going to get a breath of air." Adam jerked out of his chair and disappeared out the front door.

"Your old man has a bit of temper in him," Willie observed.

Isabel shrugged. "He has a few hot buttons. The Stanburys just happen to be one of them."

"And why is that?" For just a moment Willie appeared stone-cold sober.

"At one time he wanted to work for the palace," Isabel ad-libbed. "But, they told him he wasn't the right material, that he wasn't good enough. It's been a festering sore ever since."

She desperately hoped the story sounded plausible and reminded herself to tell Adam what she'd just told Willie. "I spoke to Shane a couple of weeks before he was killed and he mentioned somebody named Pam. Was she the tall blonde that was at the cemetery this morning?"

"Yeah, that was Pam." Willie gazed mournfully at his empty glass, then looked back at Isabel. "Shane was that gal's heart. His death near killed her."

"I'd like to talk with her. You know, extend my condolences. Do you know where I can find her?" Isabel held her breath.

Willie shrugged. "I know she's got a place close to here, but I don't know exactly where it is."

Isabel swallowed her disappointment. Willie twirled his empty glass and she gestured Bart for a refill. She'd ply Willie all night with drinks if it might get her some more information.

"Before Shane got himself killed, him and Pam spent most evenings here. I imagine eventually she'll come in," Willie said.

Eventually wasn't quick enough, Isabel thought in frustration. If her father had suffered a stroke as Meagan had said, then he needed medical attention sooner rather than later.

The rest of the evening continued to be a study in frustration. Adam rejoined Isabel and Willie and, as the hours passed, Willie introduced them to many of the tavern's regulars, but no more information about the Patriots, Shane or Pam was forthcoming.

By eight that night, Isabel had a headache from the noise and smoke and excused herself to go back to their room. Adam remained behind and she hoped desperately that on his own he could gain some clues as to where the king might be being held.

In the room, Isabel took a long, hot shower, shedding the smell of the tavern down the drain. She towel-dried, pulled on her silk nightgown and matching robe, then sat down on the edge of the bed, exhausted by the roller-coaster events of the day.

She hadn't expected everything to be quite so difficult. She'd hoped vital information would fall quickly into her lap and this whole undercover operation would be finished within a week.

Now she realized that information wasn't going to just fall into her lap. They would have to meet the right people, ask the right questions and hope for more than just a little luck.

She also hadn't considered how difficult it would be sharing intimate space with Adam. They had spent less than twenty-four hours together and already they had kissed twice. Granted, the first kiss had been necessary to establish their charade. And she suspected the second kiss had been a gesture of pity on Adam's part.

She'd been crying, half-hysterical, and he'd merely kissed her to comfort her. Even knowing the reasons for the kisses didn't negate the sweeping emotions that coursed through her when she thought of them. The truth was, she liked kissing Adam; she liked kissing him far more than she should.

She shoved these thoughts aside, disturbed that he could fill her head when she should be thinking about finding her father.

The phone on the nightstand caught her attention. She should call her mother. Since her father's kidnapping, few days went by that Isabel didn't speak to her mother.

She'd just dialed the number that would ring

Queen Josephine's private quarters when Adam returned to the room.

"I'm calling my mother," she explained.

He nodded. "I'm going to take a shower." He disappeared into the bathroom at the same time Queen Josephine answered the phone.

"Mother," Isabel said.

"Isabel...where are you? I called you today and was told you've gone into seclusion. I've been worried."

"I'm sorry, I didn't mean to worry you. Has there been any news?" Isabel heard the sound of the shower running in the bathroom and tried to shove away the picture her mind attempted to produce...a picture of a wet, naked Adam.

"No...nothing." Queen Josephine's voice was heavy with despair. "Edward isn't doing very well. I don't know what's wrong with him, perhaps the stress of taking on the throne, but he looks quite ill."

"How's Dominique?" Isabel asked, hoping to change the subject to something more pleasant. Isabel's sister Dominique's six-month pregnancy was a source of great happiness not only to Isabel and her mother, but to Stanbury supporters around the country.

"She's doing just fine." Josephine released an audible sigh. "Isabel, I haven't forgotten that you haven't answered my original question. Where exactly are you?''

Isabel was vaguely aware of the shower water turning off in the bathroom as she considered what to tell her mother. "Don't ask," she finally replied. "Mama, I can't just sit in my office and wait for others to find father."

"You aren't doing anything foolish, are you?"

Isabel looked up as Adam came out of the bathroom. He was clad only in a pair of athletic shorts and brought with him the scent of clean maleness. "Of course not," Isabel answered, unsurprised to find her mouth suddenly dry.

Had there ever been a chest so broad, so wonderfully sprinkled with just the right amount of hair and sharply defined with muscle? Isabel tore her gaze from Adam as he dropped into the chair.

"Isabel...don't get in over your head," Queen Josephine warned.

"I won't," Isabel replied, but she knew it was a lie. She was in over her head...way over her head where Adam Sinclair was concerned.

After Queen Josephine said goodbye to her eldest daughter, she moved to one of her bedroom windows. The view from this particular window was supposed to inspire peace and tranquility. The courtyard was filled with stone statues, flowers and an impressive fountain, but the view hadn't inspired peace or tranquility for her in the past three months.

"Michael, where are you?" she whispered. "You must hang on. You must be strong so you can return to me."

The news that Michael had possibly suffered a stroke while in captivity had shot waves of panic and desolation through Josephine.

She moved away from the window, her heart heavier than it had ever been. Sinking into a plush chair, her head was filled with thoughts of the man she had married thirty-three years before.

She'd only been twenty-one when she'd married him. Their marriage had been a loveless match, a political alliance between her country of Wynborough and Michael's homeland of Edenbourg. She'd met Michael on the day of her marriage to him, and had pledged her life to his for the sake of her country, and for the children she would eventually bear.

On the surface, the marriage had been a success. She and Michael had come to an understanding. He stayed busy running the country and she had her charity work and her friends. It had been a comfortable life.

Then, on the day of Michael's granddaughter's christening, Michael had disappeared. In the days that followed, Josephine had been shocked to discover the profound depth, the utter, all-encompassing love she felt for her husband.

She couldn't believe that fate would be so cruel as to open her heart to her love for Michael when it might be too late to share it with him, when she might never get the opportunity to tell him just how much she loved him.

A knock sounded at her door. "Come in," she said.

Edward Stanbury, her husband's brother, entered the room.

Josephine hadn't seen him since the day before and hoped she hid her shock at his appearance.

Since taking on the crown, Edward had aged years. His blue eyes were dull, his skin pasty white. His gray hair was limp and he appeared to have lost weight, giving him a gaunt, sick appearance.

"Is there news?" Josephine asked, rising from her chair.

He shook his head and waved her back down. "I'm afraid not. I just came by to see how you were doing." He leaned against the back of the chair directly across from where she sat.

"I think the real question should be how are you doing? Edward, you don't look well."

"I must confess, I'm not feeling very well. Perhaps I've caught a bug of some sort. Or maybe it's stress." He smiled ruefully. "After all my divorces, I thought I knew all there was to know about stress, but nothing prepared me for ruling a country." He hesitated a moment, then continued. "I'm thinking of stepping down, Josephine. I'm really not feeling well."

Josephine's mind raced, her first thought what was best for the country. If Edward relinquished the crown, then his eldest son, Luke, would be next in line. "Of course, you must do what you think best," she replied, although her heart cried out in anguish.

It should be Michael on the throne, and if not Michael, then his son, Nicholas. But, Michael was missing, and Nicholas was in hiding so everyone in the country would think him dead.

"I haven't decided yet." He frowned, looking far older than his fifty-five years. "There are so many things to consider. If only…" he allowed his voice to trail off.

Josephine could guess where his thoughts were going. "Yes, if only we could find Michael," she said, surprised to feel the burn of tears behind her eyes.

"Well, I'll see you tomorrow?" Edward said, as if he sensed her need to be alone.

"Yes."

With a nod, Edward turned and left.

Michael. Michael. Michael. Her heart cried his name in an endless litany of pain and love. Where are you? Why aren't you here with me?

He'd already missed so much. He'd been absent for Dominique's marriage to the King's High Counsel, Marcus Kent, and had missed seeing her burgeoning pregnancy. She was already through her second trimester.

Josephine frowned, a sudden thought skittering through her mind. So far Dominique had insisted nobody be told the sex of the baby she carried. Neither Dominique nor Marcus knew.

But, if the baby was a boy, with Michael and Nicholas absent, then the baby was the true heir to the Edenbourg throne. Before Edward stepped down, before Luke could step in as regent, Josephine needed to talk with Dominique.

Of course, the best possible solution was to find Michael alive and well. The tears that had burned behind her eyes now slid down her cheeks as she thought of her husband.

Please, Michael, get home safely. The country needed him. But, more importantly, she needed him.

Chapter Five

Adam sat in the back of the tavern and watched as Isabel made her way toward the bar. It was nearing closing time and Adam was tired and more than a little bit cranky.

For seven nights he'd slept in that infernal chair. And for seven days and nights he watched every man in this place lust after his "wife," and his own lust for her had grown by the minute.

Tonight she was clad in a black dress no bigger than a handkerchief. Gold chains served as the back of the dress, displaying far too much skin as far as Adam was concerned.

Beneath the chains, her skin looked creamy and smooth, and he knew every man in the pub had entertained the fantasy of touching that skin. *He'd* certainly spent far too much time indulging in sensual fantasies where she was concerned.

For the past seven days he'd seen a side of Isabel he hadn't known she possessed. She'd been good-naturedly flirtatious with the men in the tavern, and part of her allure was the fact that she seemed so genuinely unaware of her allure.

Adam frowned irritably. He certainly wasn't unaware of her allure. Her scent wrapped around him at night like a warm, sensual blanket and he was beginning to learn the little habits that made her unique.

She was cranky in the mornings, but always cheerful by the end of her first cup of coffee. She liked croissants, not toast and butter, and never jelly.

Her lower lip trembled when she was trying to hide her emotions and she always uttered a soft little sigh just before she fell into deep sleep.

For all intent and purposes, Adam had all the intimate knowledge of her that a husband would have...except he hadn't made love to her. And he suspected that's why he was feeling cranky.

Of course, he preferred to think that his crabbiness came from the fact that they hadn't gained any information in the last seven days. He preferred to believe that it was work-related frustration that gnawed at his insides and not the sufferings of sexual deprivation.

His gaze narrowed as Blake Hariman walked in. The big man with the tattooed arms scanned the room, his gaze lingering on Isabel, then moving to meet Adam's gaze. The two men held eye contact for only a long moment, then Blake broke the stare and headed back toward the billiard tables.

Adam frowned thoughtfully. He had the feeling Blake was sizing him up, but for what, Adam had no idea. Every night the two men had sat across the bar from one another, and every night Adam had felt Blake's watchful gaze on him.

He once again looked at Isabel, who was making her way back to their table clutching two drinks in her hands. As usual, her hair was puffed all out in a punky style, and her full lips were ruby-red with lipstick.

"Better drink up for strength," she said as she sat down next to him. "It's going to be a long night for you."

He knew she was referring to the fact that Bart, the owner and bartender of the place, had given Adam the job of cleaning up after hours.

The pay was cash under the table and a discount on their room. Although Isabel and Adam needed neither, it was part of the facade they wanted to maintain.

"Yeah, just think of me when you're all snuggled in bed and I'm down here slaving to keep you in cheap, tacky outfits," he said.

She laughed. "At least these cheap, tacky outfits of mine keep me blending in with the female patrons of this place."

"I suppose," he replied, his irritation rising once again. As far as he was concerned, there was no way she blended in. Throughout the past week women had come and gone from the bar, but none of them had been as pretty, as sexy or as compelling as Isabel.

"I'm beginning to think this whole scheme is nothing but a waste of our time." He scowled into his drink.

"That's not true." She leaned into him, her body warmth raising his internal temperature substantially. "We've learned about the Patriots, and we didn't know anything about them before this."

"We still don't know anything about them," Adam whispered in return. "Ben hasn't been able to find any information on them, and we sure as hell don't know if they had anything to do with your father's kidnapping."

His tone was sharp and she flinched beneath the rancor in it. Instantly he was sorry. He drew a deep breath and raked a hand through his hair, steadying himself. "I apologize. I didn't mean to yell at you. Dammit, I'm just getting frustrated."

"I know. So am I." She placed a hand on his shoulder, only serving to make matters worse.

He wondered vaguely why she couldn't sense his

simmer, smell the scent of an imminent explosion. It was growing more and more difficult to think of anything other than how badly he wanted to taste her mouth again, how much he wanted to touch her.

He eased himself away from her, grateful that she dropped her hand and straightened in her chair, taking her heat, her scent and her nearness away.

They sat side by side until closing time, sipping their drinks and playing the roles they had undertaken as Bella and Adam Wilcox.

When the bar closed, Isabel went upstairs and Adam began the task of cleaning the tables. Bart had left him alone with the instructions to clean the tables, wash any dirty glasses and sweep the floor.

Adam set to work, dreading the time when he would go upstairs to the room where Isabel slept and conform his body to what had become a torture device…that damnable lumpy chair.

He'd slept on hammocks, on the ground and on hard narrow cots, but nothing had kept sleep at bay like that chair. He wondered vaguely if his nightly restlessness was due to the lumpy stuffing of the chair or the fact that Isabel was so near, wearing that sexy lilac nightgown and a scent that drove him half wild.

How much longer could he do it? How much longer could he be tormented by Isabel and this mock marriage without overstepping the boundaries of propriety? How long could he be strong enough not to follow through on his enormous desire for her?

He'd finished with the tables and dishes and was sweeping up the floors when he heard a key in the front door. He turned, tensed and was surprised to see Blake Hariman walk in.

The big man filled the doorway and Adam eyed him warily, wondering what was going on. Was this some sort of a set-up? As Adam watched, Blake closed the door and re-locked it behind him.

Adam said nothing, but adrenaline pumped through him as he realized he should be prepared for anything. Blake walked across the room and around the back of the bar. "Buy you a drink?" he asked and placed two shot glasses and a bottle of whiskey on the bar.

"I never turn down a free drink." Adam leaned his broom against the wall and walked over to the bar, still prepared for whatever might occur.

Although Blake was big, Adam felt confident if it came to a physical altercation, Adam could take him down...unless the man had a gun, or a knife.

He watched as Blake poured two liberal shots. He picked up one as Blake picked up the other. "To your health," Blake said.

"And to yours," Adam replied. Adam threw back the drink, the whiskey burning all the way down his throat and to his stomach. "Does Bart know you help yourself to his alcohol?"

For the first time, Blake grinned. It was not a particularly pleasant gesture, as it didn't reach the cold darkness of his eyes. "Bart knows what I tell him. Nothing more, nothing less."

"Well, I appreciate the drink." Adam started back toward his broom but paused when Hariman called his name.

"Wilcox. I hear through the grapevine that you aren't much of a Stanbury supporter. Did I hear right?"

Adam kept his features schooled carefully in neutrality.

"Maybe so...maybe not, depends on who is asking and why they want to know."

Blake poured himself another shot and shrugged. "Just curious is all. There's some who think maybe it's time for some changes."

"Depends on who's making the changes," Adam answered carefully. He felt as if they were speaking in some sort of code and they had both lost the keys to exactly how the code worked.

Adrenaline still pumped through him, although he no longer anticipated a physical battle of any kind. However, he was aware that the mental game being played was every bit as dangerous as a fistfight or brawl.

"I got some friends who would like to see some changes made," Blake said, his dark gaze speculative as it lingered on Adam.

"Yeah, and I've got some friends who want to be millionaires, so what's your point?" Adam asked with more than a touch of impatience. "Look, I got work to do here." He walked over and grabbed his broom.

"Maybe my friends are actively doing things to impel change."

"So, what's that got to do with me?"

Blake shrugged his massive shoulders. "Just thought you'd like to meet some of them some time."

"Maybe," Adam replied and began to brush his broom across the floor. "As far as I'm concerned a man can't have too many friends." Adam felt the weight of Blake's gaze on him, but he didn't look up from the floor.

"I'll see if I can set something up." Blake drank the second shot then put the bottle away. Adam watched him surreptitiously, surprised to see him wash their glasses then put them away.

As Adam continued to push the broom across the floor, Blake walked to the front door. "I'll be in touch," he said, then disappeared out into the night.

Adam didn't stop sweeping until the floor was completely clean, but as he swept, his mind whirled with questions. Who, exactly, were Blake Hariman's friends? The Patriots? Or another subversive lunatic group with the desire to destroy the monarchy?

Had he just taken the first step on a journey that would lead him to the kidnapped king? Or was he on the first leg of a merry wild-goose chase that would eat up valuable time?

When he was finished with the floor, he took the stairs two at a time to the third floor, unable to staunch the flow of optimism that rushed through him.

Although he had no rational reason to think so, he couldn't help but believe that tonight's strange conversation with Blake Hariman might just be the break they had been waiting for.

He'd intended to tell Isabel the new development the moment he entered their room, but one look at her sleeping form and he didn't have the heart to wake her. Morning was soon enough to tell her the news.

Instead, he took a brief, hot shower, pulled on a pair of shorts, then left the bathroom. He stood just at the foot of the chair, then looked once again at Isabel.

She slept soundly, her breathing deep and regular. Weariness tugged at Adam's bones and he stared long and hard at the empty side of the bed.

They were two adults. She was practically engaged to another man. Surely they could share the bed for a night or two without any dire consequences.

Before giving himself a chance to think twice, he

eased down into the over-soft bed, every muscle in his body thanking him for his choice.

He was asleep almost before he closed his eyes.

Isabel was dreaming. Oh, and what a dream it was. She was dreaming of the warmth of a body spooned around the back of hers, a strong male arm thrown over her shoulder. It was the sweetest of dreams because she could decide whose body was so close to hers, whose arm was around her. And she wanted it to be Adam's body, Adam's arm.

She snuggled deeper into the dream and came fully awake. Her heart instantly worked overtime as she realized it wasn't a dream at all. It was very, very real.

Adam was in bed with her and the soft mattress had allowed their bodies to roll together in the middle of the mattress. Had he come to the bed because he was tired of sleeping in the chair, or because of his desire for her?

She didn't move, was almost afraid to continue breathing. She didn't want to wake him, didn't want to end the moment of intimate closeness.

Closing her eyes once again, she breathed in the scent of him, wishing she could turn over and he would awaken and make love to her.

Her cheeks burned at the thought and her heart raced a little faster. She hadn't made love to any man, but she knew with certainty that making love to Adam Sinclair would be a beautiful experience.

She frowned, thinking of the future her father had mapped out for her. King Michael had already made his wishes for his eldest daughter well known. He wanted her to marry Sebastian Lansbury, settle into the role of traditional wife and have lots of royal babies to continue the lineage.

But Isabel's brother Nicholas had already had one child, sweet little LeAnn. Surely he and his wife, Rebecca, would have more children...a son that would one day be the crown prince. And if they didn't have a son, it was possible Dominique's child would be a boy to continue the Stanbury lineage on the throne.

Eventually Isabel wanted children, but she didn't want to have them with Sebastian Lansbury. She certainly didn't want to marry Sebastian.

What she wanted was to remain here, in bed with Adam, forever. She could gladly spend a lifetime gazing into his fascinating gray eyes, wrapped in the warmth of his arms.

But she knew their present physical closeness wasn't due to any magic of love, but rather to the reality of physics. The mattress was soft, it was only natural their bodies had rolled together in the night.

It would be nice to believe that, out of want and need, Adam had reached for her in his sleep, but she knew better than to fall into that particular fantasy.

In fact, she knew better than to linger in this sleepy embrace, knowing there was no truth in it. Funny how that thought created an odd ache in the bottom of her heart.

The moment she moved, he awakened and rolled away from her as if she were on fire and he feared spontaneous combustion.

"Good morning," she said, hoping her face didn't radiate her dismay at how quickly he'd withdrawn from her.

"'Morning," he returned.

"I see you decided to get smart and make use of the bed."

He sat up, the sheet falling away from his naked chest. Isabel's heart raced a new kind of rhythm. How she wanted to lean forward and stroke her palm down his muscled chest, tangle her fingers in the patch of hair that was just the right amount in the center of his broad chest.

"My back couldn't handle another night on that chair," he said.

In one smooth movement he got up and out of the bed. "You know what I'd really like to do?" he asked.

Isabel's mouth went utterly dry. She certainly knew what she'd like to do. She wanted to grab hold of his hand and pull him back down to the bed with her.

She wanted him to kiss her until she lost her mind, touch her body until she was weeping with dizzying need, then take her and possess her completely.

"What?" she finally managed to ask.

"I want to get out of here."

She stared at him in confusion. "What do you mean?"

"I mean, I need to breathe some air other than what's in this room and what's in this stinking tavern. Why don't we get dressed, get some breakfast, then take off for a ride some place in the country? Just for an hour or two. What do you say?"

Energy positively rolled from him, a coiled energy that filled the room with a dangerous tension.

"Okay," she agreed.

A few moments later as she stood beneath the shower, she decided that a drive in the country sounded wonderful. Surely the time away from this room, away from the charade they were playing would make all the crazy thoughts she'd been having about Adam fly right out of her head.

They walked to their usual café for coffee and croissants, then left the café and walked to where Adam had parked his car on the first night he'd arrived at the King's Men Tavern.

Adam was quiet through breakfast and during

their drive. The June air drifted into the open car windows, banishing any lingering scent of the pub from Isabel's mind.

It was a gorgeous day and Isabel hadn't realized until this moment how tightly confined their lives had been for the past seven days. They had spent far too many hours cooped up in their tiny room, then enclosed in the smoky, noisy interior of the bar.

With each mile that passed, Adam seemed to relax. The tension she'd felt rolling from him since the moment he'd opened his eyes that morning disappeared and his fingers beat a faint rhythm on the steering wheel, as if music filled his head.

"Beautiful, isn't it?" He finally broke the silence and swept a hand out to encompass their surroundings.

Isabel gazed out the window at the lush, green fields. In the distance a bright blue lake sparkled in the sunshine. Her heart expanded with love, with the joy of her country. "As far as I'm concerned, there is no place prettier than Edenbourg. My father used to tell me it was the precious jewel of the North Sea."

She sighed wistfully. "I'd give all the wealth in the Chamber of Riches to hear him say those words again."

Adam shot her a curious glance. "I always

thought the Chamber of Riches was just a rumor, that it didn't really exist.''

"It exists," Isabel replied. "Although I don't know its location." The Chamber of Riches was a secret vault that contained the wealth amassed by the Stanbury monarchy over centuries. "Only the king knows how to get into the Chamber of Riches."

They drove a little further, then to Isabel's surprise, Adam turned down a narrow lane that led to an attractive cottage.

"What's this?" she asked as he parked the car in front of the place.

A curtain at one of the front windows fluttered and a moment later the front door opened and Nicholas stood on the threshold.

"Nicholas!" Isabel flew from the car at the sight of her brother. She hadn't seen him since the insiders at the palace had orchestrated his "kidnapping" and circulated the rumor of his death.

"Nicholas, it's so good to see you," she said as he embraced her. She was vaguely aware of Adam joining them at the door.

"And it's a shock to see you." Nicholas hugged her, then held her by the shoulders and eyed her from head to toe. "What on earth have you done to yourself?"

"Why don't we talk about it inside?" Adam suggested.

"Of course," Nicholas said and together the three of them entered the small house.

Inside, Nicholas's wife Rebecca and the baby LeAnn greeted them. Isabel hugged her sister-in-law tightly while LeAnn gurgled in her playpen with excitement.

Within minutes, the four of them were seated around a wooden table, drinking coffee and catching up on all the news.

LeAnn sat on her mother's lap, happily entertained with a ring of plastic keys.

"How long have you been here?" Isabel asked.

"Not long," Nicholas replied. "We're moved on a regular basis."

"The country is mourning your death." Isabel studied her handsome brother with his dark hair and blue eyes. He wore the stress of the past few months. He appeared thinner and new lines creased his forehead.

"Obviously there are some people who are not mourning, but rather celebrating." The lines in his forehead deepened.

Isabel reached for his hand across the table. "The majority of Edenbourg mourns. The people long to have father and you back in your rightful positions." She released his hand as he nodded.

"So, what are you two up to? What's going on and why are you dressed like that?"

Quickly Isabel told Nicholas and Rebecca what

she and Adam were doing. "Unfortunately, we haven't gained much information so far," she finished.

"Actually, I have a little more to add," Adam said. Isabel listened in astonishment as Adam told them what had transpired the night before between him and Blake Hariman.

Hope soared inside her. Finally...finally they were making some headway. "Why didn't you tell me this earlier?" she asked when he'd finished.

"I'm telling you now." His voice was even, but his eyes held an intensity she didn't quite understand. It was the same look he'd had when he'd told her he needed to get out of the room, get away from the tavern for a little while.

"What other news is there?" Nicholas asked, seemingly unaware of any tension.

"When I spoke to mother last night, she mentioned that Edward is ill and is thinking perhaps it best if he cede the crown."

Nicholas frowned. "And that means unless we can untangle all this mess, Luke will take on the mantle of kingship."

"And I'm not sure I trust him," Isabel said.

Rebecca looked at her, her brown eyes widening in surprise. "Why? According to what I heard, he saved your life by shooting Shane Moore."

"I know." Isabel didn't know why she didn't particularly care for her cousin Luke. Luke was outgoing and charming and obviously doted on his father. But, there had been occasions when Isabel thought she'd smelled alcohol on his breath at times of the day when drinking would have been inappropriate.

She sighed. "I just wish we could find Father and everything could go back to the way it was."

"I just hope we find Father before it's too late," Nicholas said softly. Rebecca reached out and took her husband's hand. Their love for one another was obvious and caused a wistful ache inside Isabel.

"It's already too late for things to go back to the way they were," Rebecca said.

"What do you mean?" Isabel looked at her sister-in-law curiously.

Rebecca smiled sadly. "We've all changed with this experience. The whole country will have changed. One of the things that made me fall in love with Edenbourg was that it seemed to be a country with no fear, there was an innocence. We will have lost that."

It wasn't until they were leaving the cottage that Isabel thought of Rebecca's words. It was true. This experience had changed them all already. And with a start, she realized she'd changed in the course of the past week.

She'd always believed her job in the Ministry of Defense was enough for her. She'd never particularly felt the need to marry or have children.

But, seeing the obvious depth of love between Nicholas and Rebecca, seeing LeAnn as the product of that love, had stirred a depth of yearning inside Isabel that she hadn't known existed.

She suddenly realized she wanted what Nicholas and Rebecca had…that sweeping passion, that committed, forever kind of love. She wanted to be a wife…and a mother. And she wanted it with Lieutenant Commander Adam Sinclair.

Chapter Six

On the way back, they stopped at a small café for lunch.

"How did you know where Nicholas was?" Isabel asked as they waited for their orders.

"Ben told me," Adam explained. "We figured Prince Nicholas would want to be kept apprised of what we were doing and might be hungry for news from the palace."

"He looked tired."

Adam nodded. "Yes, he did." He paused to take a sip of his water. "This has got to be hard on him. From what I understand, he, Rebecca and LeAnn are being moved about every week or so to ensure their anonymity and safety."

"At least they have each other to cling to," Isabel said, remembering the gentle touch of their hands, the look of intense love that had flowed from her brother to his wife. "That has to be an enormous comfort."

She opened her napkin and placed it on her lap, her thoughts still filled with the couple they had just left. Once again a yearning filled her and she felt as if she had a hole in her soul.

"Nicholas looks at her as if his world begins and ends with her, and she looks at him the same way. Love can be so beautiful."

One of Adam's dark eyebrows rose slightly. "I've never heard you express such sentimentality before."

She felt a blush warm her face and at the same time his words somehow made her angry. It was as if he were negating a vital dimension of her heart, the very feminine part of her.

She leaned forward. "Just because I don't talk about it doesn't mean I don't feel things like that," she exclaimed vehemently. "I don't think there is anything as beautiful in the world as the kind of love that lasts a lifetime."

"Okay," he said slowly, as if surprised by her outburst.

At that moment the waitress appeared with their orders. As she served them, Isabel gathered her thoughts, wanting Adam to understand the transformations she felt had occurred inside her.

"I think maybe you were right when you said I was somehow trying to prove something to my father," she began when the waitress had once again departed from their table. "When we started this whole undercover business, I wanted to show him that I was smart enough, strong enough and good enough to save him. I wanted him to realize that he'd made a mistake when he forced me to give up my military career. Now none of that seems important anymore. I just want to find him because I love him, because Nicholas and Dominique love him and because my mother is absolutely heartbroken without him."

"And because the country needs him," Adam added.

For some reason, his words once again irritated her. "It isn't always about the country." She sat back in her chair and eyed him intently, deciding now was the time to ask him what she'd wanted to know for some time. "Do you have a woman in your life, Adam? Is there somebody special?"

His eyes were dark opaque clouds, impossible to see behind. "No, there's nobody special. I'm not looking for anyone special." He picked up his water glass and took a sip, then continued. "I guess I'm like my father in that respect. My career is my wife, my lover…my life."

"Don't you ever get lonely? Don't you ever have moments when you wish there was somebody who knew you so well, loved you so much they could guess your thoughts and share your most secret of dreams?"

He didn't answer for a moment and his gaze was transfixed on his plate. "Sure, I suppose there are times I get lonely, but the feeling passes quickly enough."

He looked at her once again. "I was born to be a military man, not a husband or a father. Just like you were born a princess and will do what's best for Edenbourg. Eventually you will follow your father's wishes and marry Sebastian Lansbury."

Shock riveted through Isabel. She had no idea he even knew who Sebastian Lansbury was. She certainly hadn't considered that he thought she was going to marry the fop. "I am not marrying that man," she protested.

It was his turn to look at her in surprise. "But, I thought you were engaged to him."

"I'm engaged to nobody," she exclaimed vehemently. "And if I have my way, I'll never be engaged to that pompous Sebastian."

"But, the newspapers…"

"…lie," she interjected.

"I wondered how he was taking your disappearance, if he was upset since you've been in 'seclusion.'"

"The only disappearance that would upset Sebastian is if he looked in the mirror and didn't see

the reflection of the person he loves more than anything in the world," she said dryly.

Adam laughed. The sound was deep and attractive and Isabel realized she didn't think she'd ever
heard him really laugh before. It sent a wave of
wonderful warmth flooding through her.

They ate for a few minutes in silence. Isabel's
mind refused to stop working, filtering thoughts and
emotions that were new...alien to her.

Born a princess. Adam's words whirled around
and around in her head. She was a princess and
Adam seemed confident she'd make her decisions
based on what was best for the country...that she
would follow her father's wishes without rebellion.

"Sometimes I wish I really was Bella Wilcox,"
she said aloud.

Again one of Adam's eyebrows raised. "Why on
earth would you wish that?"

Isabel frowned and set down her fork. "A
woman like Bella can follow her heart no matter
where it leads her. She doesn't have to worry about
the duty or the responsibility of a title. She doesn't
have to please a country, she only has to please
herself."

Adam gazed at her for a long moment, then
looked down at his plate. "We'd better finish eating
and get back to the tavern," he finally said.

It wasn't the response she wanted from him, but
she wasn't sure what she wanted from him. Some-

how, what had begun as a simple covert plan to find her father had gotten far more complicated.

They finished eating, returned to the tavern and resumed their role-playing. As they sat at a table, visiting with the people they had come to know, Isabel's mind continued to race, this time with the information of Adam's meeting with Blake Hariman.

Every time the door opened, she prayed it would be Blake or one of his cohorts coming to talk to Adam. She hoped that the "friends" Blake had talked about were the Patriots and that those people were the ones responsible for her father's kidnapping.

She was aware of time ticking by, aware that the longer it took, the lower were the odds that her father would be alive and well. He'd already had one stroke without medical attention. What if he had another? Her heart beat a dull thud. What if it was already too late?

She mentally shook the thought out of her head. She couldn't believe that. Surely if her father had suffered a massive stroke and had died, somebody would be talking, the news would be out somehow.

"I'm going to run up to the room and get a couple of aspirins," Adam said. "I'll be right back."

She nodded her assent. It was just after 8:00 p.m., and she knew his headache was probably due to the incessant noise and smoke.

He'd just disappeared up the staircase when somebody tapped on Isabel's shoulder. She turned, a wave of shock suffusing her as she saw Pam Sommersby.

"Take a walk with me." The blonde's brown eyes held the skittish fear of a wild animal, but implored Isabel to do as she bid.

Without hesitation, Isabel slid off her chair and followed just behind the tall, buxom woman. It was only when they reached the door of the tavern that she thought of Adam, wanted to wait for him to join them.

Pam seemed to know her thoughts. "Just the two of us. Nobody else," she said, then disappeared out the door.

Isabel hurried after her. She wasn't about to let this opportunity slip away just because Adam had a headache. She had no other choice but to follow.

Although she was eager, she wasn't stupid. She knew she could be walking into a trap of some sort and was mentally on guard.

When she stepped outside the tavern, nobody appeared to be hiding in the shadows except Pam, who motioned for her to walk with her.

They walked a block without speaking. Isabel wanted to ask a million questions, but held her tongue, afraid of scaring Pam off.

And she looked as if she could be scared off quite easily. Her gaze darted from one point to another with frantic speed and she appeared ready to bolt at any minute.

They walked for another block before they came to a bench at a bus stop. Pam sat and motioned Isabel next to her. "I know who you are," Pam said, her voice low and slightly unsteady.

"Bella, I'm Bella Wilcox," Isabel said. "Shane was my cousin on my mother's side."

Pam shook her head, her gaze intent on Isabel. "No. I know for a fact that Shane didn't have any cousins. I know you're Princess Isabel. Despite your hair and makeup and clothing, I recognize you."

Isabel opened her mouth to protest, to bluff her way through, then changed her mind. "Yes, I am."

Tears filled Pam's eyes and she wrung the strap of the straw purse she carried. "I'm sorry. I'm so sorry." The tears tumbled from her eyes and spilled down her cheeks. "I didn't know...I truly didn't know everything that Shane was involved with. I swear I didn't know that people would get kidnapped or hurt."

Isabel believed her. It was impossible to look into those tearful brown eyes and not see the heart inside the woman. "Why did you run from us on the day of the funeral?" she asked.

Pam pulled a crumpled tissue from her purse and swiped at her tears. "I was so upset, and I was frightened. Everything went so crazy. Shane was dead, and I'd heard that your brother was also dead." Tears once again poured from her eyes. "I loved Shane, but I had no idea what he'd done...what he was responsible for."

Isabel wanted to hate her. She wanted to hate the woman who had loved the man who had kidnapped her father, but try as she might, she could find no hate in her heart.

"Why did you come to speak to me now?" Isabel asked.

Again Pam dabbed at her eyes, then drew in a deep shuddering breath. "Because too many people have died already. Because this has gotten out of control and has to end before more people die."

Isabel took one of Pam's hands in hers. "We have to find my father. We've received word that he's had a stroke...is ill. Can you tell me where he's being held?"

"I'm sorry. I can't. I don't know." The words escaped her as mournful as a moan. "I think only a couple of people know exactly where he's being held. Shane was the one in charge of that and now he's dead."

"Was Shane the mastermind behind all of this?"

Pam shook her head, her long blond hair swaying around her face. "No. Somebody else was helping Shane. Somebody in the palace."

Isabel released Pam's hand and leaned back against the bench, frustration tearing at her insides.

They had suspected there was a traitor in the palace, but who? Who had something to gain by kidnapping the king?

"Somewhere, somebody has to know where my father is," she finally said.

Pam was silent for a long moment and again her fingers twisted the strap of her purse. "Somebody in the group would know."

"The group? You mean the Patriots?"

"No. Shane had nothing but scorn for the Patriots. He said they were nothing but a bunch of whiners with no backbone."

"Then what group?" Isabel asked.

Pam said. "The Frees."

"Do you know who they are? How we can get to them?"

Pam hesitated, then nodded. She looked at Isabel, her eyes holding a touch of fear. "They are dangerous people, Your Highness."

Isabel held her gaze intently. "They have my father. Pam, whatever political beliefs you might hold, whatever agenda you might have…you have to help me. I beg you…my father's very life might depend on it."

Again Pam was silent for a long moment. She tilted her head back and looked up, as if she might find answers in the starry sky overhead. Isabel held her breath, wanting to shake her, to slap her, somehow force her to do something…anything to help.

"Okay," she finally said. "I'll do what I can. I know when they meet and where. They trust me. I could bring you and the man who is pretending to be your husband to one of their meetings."

Tears burned at Isabel's eyes, tears of gratitude. Closer...surely they were getting closer to success. "Thank you," she said.

Pam nodded and stood, as if suddenly eager to be away. "Tuesday night, meet me here. I'll take you where you want to go." She started to walk away.

"Pam?" Isabel called softly.

The tall blonde turned back to her. "How did you know it was me?"

For the first time a smile curved Pam's lips, the gesture making her quite pretty. "I was six years old when you were born. It probably sounds silly to you, but I pretended that you were my baby sister. I've followed your life, read every news article and seen most every picture ever taken of you." Pam's smile fell away. "Anyway, I recognized you the moment I saw you."

"Should I be concerned about others being able to recognize me?" Isabel asked.

"No, I think you're safe. You sure don't look like yourself in that getup." She drew a deep breath. "I'll see you here Tuesday night, at 10:00 p.m." With these words she hurried off, quickly swallowed up by the night.

Tuesday night. Only two more days, Isabel thought. She looked up at the night sky and sent a prayer heavenward, then turned and began to walk briskly back to the tavern.

Two more days and Pam could help her and Adam infiltrate the group responsible for her father's kidnapping.

She only hoped her father could last another two days. She prayed it wasn't already too late to save him.

Adam was beyond frantic.

He'd come downstairs from their room to find Isabel nowhere in sight. At first he hadn't been concerned. He'd assumed she was probably in the ladies' room.

When enough time had passed that he thought she should have returned, the first edge of panic crawled into the pit of his belly.

He'd asked Bart if he'd seen where she'd gone, had even asked one of the women patrons to check the women's restroom. But Isabel was nowhere to be found and nobody had seen where she had gone.

As the minutes ticked by, dreadful thoughts filled his head: Had somebody seen beneath the makeup and vivid hair color? Had somebody seen beyond the crazy clothes and recognized the princess beneath?

His heart banged painfully into his ribs at this

thought. Had she been kidnapped? Taken to the same place where her father was being held?

He'd stood outside on the sidewalk and looked first one way, then the other. There was no way to know which direction to go, where to even begin to search for her. He'd gone back inside, once again checking every nook and cranny of the tavern.

Panic roared through him. Was she hurt? He knew Isabel wouldn't have gone willingly with anyone. She would have kicked and fought like a wild woman. He knew how well versed she was in hand-to-hand combat. She'd excelled at self-defense techniques while in military training.

But, if somebody had slipped some sort of drug into her drink, or if they'd somehow managed to sneak up behind her, she could have been taken down easily. And even though everyone he asked professed to have seen nothing, Adam trusted no person in the dive.

The panic he'd tried to tamp down exploded inside him. He would never forgive himself if something had happened to her. He should have never agreed to this crazy scheme in the first place.

He was just about to decide that he needed to call the palace and send for help when she walked through the door. Her cheeks were flushed with pretty color and her eyes sparkled brightly.

And the sight of her, seemingly oblivious to his worry, both relieved and enraged him.

The moment she stepped into the door he grabbed her by one arm. "Where in the hell have you been?" he demanded, wanting nothing more than to take her by the shoulders and shake her senseless.

"I went for a walk," she said slowly.

He stared at her in disbelief. "A walk? You went for a walk?" The urge to shake her grew stronger, but more than that, he wanted to grab her to his chest and hold her tightly, assure himself that she was truly all right.

And this need only made him more angry. "You went for a walk without me? Just got a crazy impulse and took off? What in the hell were you thinking?" he thundered.

"Adam, let's talk about it upstairs." She tried to pull her arm out of his grasp, but he refused to release her. "Everyone is looking at us," she said, the color in her cheeks intensifying.

"Give him hell, honey!" One of the working girls yelled from someplace nearby.

The feminine voice made Adam realize they had drawn the attention of everyone in the place. Still firmly holding on to her, he headed for the stairs.

As they started up the stairs, hoots and hollers followed them, the men yelling for Adam to take control of his wayward wife, and the women shouting their support for Isabel.

Adam was only vaguely aware of their jeers and

cheers. The anger that roared through him was like a wild animal clawing at his insides.

He had no idea why or where she had disappeared to, but the fact that she had taken such a chance in going out alone, had not given a moment's thought to how he might react to her disappearance, shot a red-hot fury through him.

He didn't release his hold on her until they were in their room, then he slammed the door and faced her. "What in God's name were you thinking? You took a walk?" He eyed her in utter astonishment. "Do you have any idea what kind of a risk you took in going off alone? I was just about to call the palace and tell them to send out the royal security."

"I'm sorry, but it couldn't be helped."

"The hell it couldn't," he exploded. "Have you forgotten that you are a princess? That the people who kidnapped your father would probably love to add you to their lair as well? You might want to be Bella Wilcox, but you aren't and you can't just go running off alone."

She sank down onto the edge of the bed, her short skirt riding precariously up, exposing her silky, shapely thighs. For just a brief moment as Adam stared at her, he momentarily forgot why he was so angry.

He wanted her. How he wanted her. His anger was overridden by the stronger emotion of lust. A shudder worked through him as he fought to control the want and instead attempted to refocus on his ire.

"What in the world was so important that you had to leave without me?"

She jumped up and walked toward him until she stood toe-to-toe with him, a flame of answering anger igniting in her eyes. "If you'd stop yelling at me for a minute, I'd tell you where I went."

Her mouth was mere inches from his and suddenly Adam was no longer in control. Anger merged with desire, relief combined with want. He grabbed her by the shoulders and pulled her roughly against him as his mouth sought hers with ravenous hunger.

Her response was instantaneous. She looped her arms around his neck, leaned into him and returned the kiss with a hunger to match his own.

The world seemed to pause. Anger fell aside, royal intrigue was forgotten, as the kiss deepened...and lingered. Adam worked his hands up her back, then lightly touched the sides of her breasts. He felt almost light-headed, dizzied by the intimate contact.

She leaned back to allow him to touch her even more intimately. As his hands came into full contact with her breasts, she moaned into his mouth. The hardness of her nipples pressed up through the material to meet the heat of his hands. She moaned again. The sound of her pleasure swept pleasure through him.

As he thought of all that could have happened to her, that she might have been kidnapped—or worse—while out on her own, a moan slid from his throat.

"You have no idea what you put me through," he said as he broke the kiss and moved his lips to the sweet-smelling skin just beneath her ear. "You have no idea what kind of fear went through me."

She pulled back from him, her eyes glazed with desire. She grabbed one of his hands and tugged him toward the bed. "Show me, Adam. Show me how glad you are that I'm all right. Make love to me."

Her words doused him with cold reality, and he stepped back from her, his anger returning tenfold. "Of course I'm glad that you are all right. I've already got one black mark against my name. If anything happens to you, I'd be held accountable."

The beautiful light in her eyes dimmed with each word he spoke. Once again she sat on the bed and this time he kept his gaze carefully focused away from her sexy legs. He also desperately tried to put out of his head the fact that she'd just asked him to make love to her.

But the pain in her eyes haunted him. He swept a hand across his jaw, wanting to take away that pain. "Isabel," he said softly. "We can't get caught up in this fantasy we're living right now. We are not Bella and Adam Wilcox. And, no matter how difficult this all gets, you can't ever forget that you are Princess Isabel.''

He frowned. He had no right to kiss Princess Isabel, much less make love to her. Yes, it was important that she not forget who she was…but it was more important that he didn't forget who he was…Adam Sinclair, the son of a traitor.

Chapter Seven

"I can't help but think if we can figure out who stands to gain by my father's kidnapping, then we'll know who the insider is at the palace," Isabel said.

She and Adam were in their room, waiting for the time they would meet Pam and infiltrate the group that was responsible for the actual kidnapping of King Michael. But, what Isabel wanted was the person who was at the heart of the treachery, the mastermind behind it all.

"We've gone over this before," Adam said as he paced the small confines of the room. As usual, he looked like a restless lion passively rebelling against the confines of a cage.

"But, we've got to be missing something," she replied.

For the past two days, ever since she'd thrown herself at him, asked him to make love to her and he had responded so coldly, they had endured a cool distance between each other.

It was a distance broken only when they played their roles of Adam and Bella Wilcox, and in the unconsciousness of sleep.

Adam had rejected the chair in favor of the bed for sleeping. At night, they got beneath the covers, careful not to touch one another, careful not to in any way cross the invisible barrier of personal space.

But, in sleep, they found one another. His arm would curl around her, or her leg would fold across one of his. It was as if in unconsciousness, their bodies hungered for one another, their skin sought the touch of the other.

Each and every inadvertent physical contact suffered during the day was a torture for Isabel. If his hand brushed against hers, her heart leapt in response. If his shoulder bumped against hers, she felt a tingling jolt clear down to her toes.

"The first person who would have the most to gain would be Nicholas. With your father gone, he becomes king," Adam said, not halting his rapid pace back and forth in front of her.

"But we know Nicholas wasn't involved because they kidnapped Ben impersonating Nicholas," Isabel replied. "Besides, Nicholas would never do anything to hurt Father."

Adam stopped pacing and nodded. He raked a hand across his jaw, as always looking surprised to feel the growth of whiskers on his chin. "I agree. Prince Nicholas is a good man. And that leaves the next in line to succeed, your Uncle Edward."

Isabel frowned thoughtfully, trying to stay focused on the conversation and not remember the absolute wonder of awakening in Adam's arms. "I just can't believe Uncle Edward would be behind all this. He returned to Edenbourg after years in the States because he wanted to reconcile differences between himself and my father. I can't fathom that he returned here to have my father and my brother kidnapped so he could be king."

Adam finally stopped his pacing and sank into the chair. His eyes were dark, hooded as he looked at her. "That scenario is especially difficult to believe since Edward's talking about stepping down already."

"And Luke would be next in line for the crown." Isabel thought of her cousin. "But, it seems so far-fetched to think that a man who is fourth in the succession line would go to all this trouble. I mean, how could Luke know his father would get ill and relinquish the crown?"

"I agree. Edward is a relatively young man. What is he, mid fifties?" Isabel nodded and Adam continued. "It's conceivable that Edward could have reigned for the next twenty-five or thirty years."

"A long time for a mastermind to wait for his reward," Isabel replied.

"I agree." Adam looked at his watch. "It's time."

Isabel's heart jumped. It was time. Time to meet Pam. Time to infiltrate the group that had kidnapped her father. She hoped...prayed that by the end of this night they would have some answers. She stood and together they started for the door.

"Bella and Adam Wilcox are now on stage," Adam murmured and grabbed her hand.

He held her hand as they made their way through the crowded bar. Isabel loved the way his hand felt around hers. So big and strong, so utterly masculine.

He released hers only when they stepped outside and started up the street in the direction of the bus stop where they were to meet Pam.

The moment he let go of her hand, she felt bereft, and it was at that moment she realized the depth of her love for Lieutenant Commander Adam Sinclair.

She loved him as she'd never loved anyone before in her life. She loved him with a depth and breadth that nearly stole her breath away. The realization struck her like a lightning bolt jolting through her and she stumbled. Adam grabbed her to keep her from falling on her face.

"All right?" he asked, his gorgeous gray eyes as unreadable as ever.

She nodded, afraid if she spoke she'd blurt out her love for him. He dropped his hands and they continued on their way, Isabel's heart like a hundred-pound stone in her chest.

She loved him. She had loved him years ago when she'd been a raw recruit and he'd been her commanding officer. At that time she'd known that to push the issue might destroy his career.

But, now the obstacle was no longer their careers. The real obstacle was his heart, and it was obvious that as much as she loved him, he didn't...or wouldn't...love her back.

"You okay?" His low voice broke into her thoughts.

No, I'm not okay. I'm in love with you and I don't know what to do about it. I love you and my heart is breaking into tiny pieces. "Sure, I'm fine," she replied. "A little nervous," she admitted.

"A little nervous is good. A little nervous means you understand that what we are about to do is dangerous. A little nervous will keep you on your toes and thinking clearly."

"Are you nervous?" she asked.

He shot her a quicksilver smile that warmed her heart. "A little."

Pam was already at the bus stop and when she saw them she hurried toward them. "I hope I'm doing the right thing," she said worriedly after Isabel introduced Adam.

"Of course you are," Adam said, his tone gentle. "You are absolutely doing the right thing, not only for Princess Isabel, but for the country."

His words and kind tone seemed to calm Pam, and Isabel only loved him more for knowing instinctively what the fragile woman needed at the moment.

"Then I guess we're off. It's a bit of a walk, but nobody drives to the meetings."

They walked four blocks with nobody saying a word. Isabel had never been in this particular part of Edenbourg before. Most of the businesses were closed, their windows broken or boarded up. The houses were small, unkempt. Neglect and abandonment was everywhere.

"You haven't been able to remember anything that Shane said as to where the king is being held?" Adam asked softly as they walked.

Pam shook her head in obvious frustration. "I've done nothing for the past two days but rack my brain for anything that might help you. The only thing I ever heard Shane say was once I heard him on the phone telling somebody that the king bee was hidden in the honeycomb."

"The honeycomb? What could that mean?" Isabel asked.

Pam shrugged. "I don't know. Maybe nothing. Maybe it was just an expression Shane used, and it doesn't mean anything at all."

"You can't remember anything else?" Adam pressed.

"Sorry." Her expression mirrored her regret. "But, if I do, I'll tell you. Now, no more talking. We're nearly there."

They walked another half a block, then left the street and made their way through tangled underbrush on the property of an old abandoned church.

Pam led them to the back of the church where the door hung askew, held to the rotting wood by a single, rusty hinge.

Graffiti defaced the exterior walls of the old building and Isabel's heart ached as she thought of her father held in a place as dismal or more dismal than this.

If there was a meeting going on, it was a quiet one, Isabel thought. Inside the church the only audible sound was their footsteps crunching the broken glass and garbage that littered the floor. It looked as if nobody had been in the place for years.

For the first time Isabel wondered if Pam was leading them into a trap. Was Pam truly a rebel's grieving lover attempting to undo what had been done? Or was she a rabid revolutionary intent on ridding the world of all the Stanburys?

Isabel looked at Adam and he must have seen in her eyes a flicker of her sudden doubt and fear. He reached for her hand while his other hand moved to his waist. She knew he had a gun tucked beneath his belt and hidden by the large T-shirt that was untucked.

Pam led them through what had once been the sanctuary and was now filled with trash and broken wooden pews. The evening sky was visible through a hole in the ceiling.

"This way," Pam said, motioning them to follow her into what had once been the small vestry. No longer did the room hold sacred robes and items. The shelves that lined one of the walls were all empty.

Adam and Isabel watched in amazement as Pam swung the bookshelves out to reveal a set of concrete stairs leading down.

"A bunker?" Adam asked, his voice holding amazement.

"That's right. It's an old World War II bunker," Pam said. "We've all been meeting here for the past year and a half."

As they descended the concrete steps, again a million doubts assailed Isabel's mind. She was grateful that Adam still held her hand. As Pam reached to open the door that would take them into the bunker, Isabel squeezed Adam's hand.

They were about to find out if Pam was a friend, or if she was a very clever insurgent who had fooled them both.

Adam had not relaxed since the moment they had arrived. The "group" consisted of about twenty people, mostly men. The instant they had stepped into the concrete bunker, Adam had felt the thick tension of suspicion...a suspicion that had been dispelled when Pam had introduced them as Shane's cousin and her husband.

Apparently Pam's endorsement and the familial connection to Shane Moore had been enough to allay distrust. They were accepted without further question.

Still, Adam had remained on guard throughout the meeting. The cold metal of the gun in his waistband had been a small comfort as he realized probably half the men in the room were carrying.

During the actual meeting, there was no mention of the imprisoned king. What there was, was a lot of long-winded rhetoric and political pipe dreams. First one, then another stood to vent frustrations and demand that it was time for change. Adam found the speeches boring, the men zealous and the whole atmosphere disturbing.

Officially, the business of the meeting was now

over, but most had lingered to mingle and make small talk. He and Isabel had remained, hoping to learn something of significance.

Adam kept Isabel at his side, an arm thrown territorially around her shoulder. He tried to ignore the heady scent of her, and the way her bare arm felt beneath his fingertips. Instead he tried to stay focused on how difficult this particular ordeal had to be on her.

Not only was she hoping somebody would say something that would lead them to her father, but she was also listening to a lot of anti-Stanbury sentiment.

He scanned the room, trying to discern the pecking order within the group. So far it had been difficult to figure out who was the boss...who exactly was in control.

Several of the males were loud and verbose on the subject of, the country needing change, but Adam suspected they were merely minions with mouths and no control. Adam had a feeling the real leader of this band was probably one of the men who had sat through the official meeting saying nothing.

He dropped his arm to his side as Isabel stepped a few feet away to speak with Pam. He let her go reluctantly, but knew to do anything else might be suspect.

The king bee is in the honeycomb. The words

Pam had heard Shane tell somebody replayed in his head. What might it mean? Was it simply a way of Shane telling the mastermind that they had the king under lock and key, or did the sentence hold a clue to exactly where the king was being kept?

And who in the hell had Shane been talking to? Adam knew that every member of the staff and family had been checked and double-checked and all had passed with flying colors.

What concerned him most was that he suspected Isabel had come to this meeting tonight hoping to get answers. Adam knew the operation of infiltrating and gaining trust in this group would take time…precious time that they might not have in order to save King Michael's life.

The other concern he had was how long he could continue to be strong where Isabel was concerned. He watched her now as she spoke with Pam. Her lovely face was animated and he could tell she was fully immersed in the role of Bella.

But, Adam saw cracks in the facade. There was a new pain reflected in the depths of her green eyes, a pain he feared he was partially responsible for. But he'd had no choice.

He knew he'd devastated her by rejecting her plea for him to make love to her, but what other option had there been? If he had made love to Isabel, the inevitable outcome would have been heartache.

There was no way he believed that she was in love with him. She'd gotten caught up in the crazy fantasy of their pretend marriage, was having problems separating herself from Bella.

When this was all over, she'd once again be Princess Isabel and eventually Adam knew she would marry the man chosen for her. It would be a royal match with all the pomp and circumstance the country and her father required. There was no place in Princess Isabel's future for him.

But, that didn't stop him from wanting her and he wasn't sure how long he could keep up the husband and wife charade without making a mistake that would only make their eventual parting more difficult.

It was after midnight when they finally left the bunker and headed back to the King's Men Tavern. Pam split from them at the bus stop, telling them that she would be in touch before the next meeting.

"Nothing," Isabel exclaimed as she and Adam walked down the darkened streets. "The whole night was a stupid waste of time."

"Isabel, we couldn't very well ask questions without drawing unwanted attention and suspicion to ourselves. It's going to take time to gain the right people's trust. Unfortunately, there's just no way to hurry things."

"I know." She caught her bottom lip between her teeth, looking far younger than her twenty-eight years. Adam fought the impulse to take her in her arms and hold her close to comfort her.

He knew what she was thinking. Time was running out for her father. The truth was, time might have already run out for the king.

"I can't go on." Edward eased into a chair in Queen Josephine's living room, his son Luke at attention just behind him. "I'm sick, and I'm not getting better."

"What does the doctor say?" Josephine asked, concerned as she realized that every day Edward looked more and more ill. Over the past three and a half months, she'd grown rather fond of Edward, who seemed to be a man who'd finally outgrown the wildness of his youth. She knew he'd tried to be a support to her through the trials of the events that had rocked the country.

"He thinks it's stress-related. All I know is I'm so weary it's hard to think. And Edenbourg needs more than I can give at this time." Edward raked a hand wearily across his forehead, looking as if the effort of the minimal act had exhausted him.

Luke Stanbury placed a hand on his father's shoulder and frowned at Josephine. "I've tried to convince him just to take a vacation, to get away and give himself some time to get back on his feet."

Edward shook his head and smiled faintly up at

his eldest son, then looked back at Josephine. "This country doesn't need a vacationing king. There has been too much turmoil since Michael's kidnapping. The country needs stability and I'm afraid I can't be what is needed at this time."

"Edward, I've told you before. You must do what is best for you, and I will support whatever decision you make." Although Josephine meant what she said, her heart cried out at the thought of yet another man sitting on the throne where her Michael should be.

"Then it's settled," Edward said. "On the last Saturday of this month, there will be a coronation crowning Luke King of Edenbourg."

"A coronation?" Josephine looked at him in surprise. It was one thing for Luke to act as king in Michael's absence, quite another to be proclaimed the one and true king of the country.

"It's time, Josephine," Edward said with obvious pain in his eyes. "The country has been floundering for too long. It is time for somebody to step up and take control."

"I've tried to talk some sense into him," Luke said helplessly.

"The country needs a real king," Edward said adamantly.

He rose from his chair, as did Josephine.

"Before that happens, I hope we find Uncle Michael alive and well," Luke said somberly as he stood close enough to Edward that the older man could lean on him.

Josephine nodded, her emotions rising precariously close to the surface. "As I said, I will support whatever is in the best interest of Edenbourg."

As they reached the door, Edward leaned forward and kissed her softly on the cheek. "I grieve with you," he said softly. She knew he was not only talking about Michael's kidnapping, but also about Nicholas's reported death.

Josephine nodded, grateful when Edward and Luke left her alone.

She wanted to cry, but felt as if her body had been wrung dry by all the tears she'd cried over the past weeks. Her heart rebelled at the thought of Luke as king. In spite of his charm and his obvious devotion to Edward, Josephine didn't particularly care for her nephew.

It was nothing she could put her finger on, just a feeling she had. But, she no longer trusted her own feelings, for all of them were so intricately tied to Michael and his absence from her life.

She wasn't sure if she disliked Luke for genuine reasons or because she'd somehow unconsciously known when Edward became acting king that eventually, if Michael wasn't found and Nicholas remained in hiding, then Luke would be the one sitting on the throne.

Unless Dominique was carrying a boy. If the

child she carried was a son, then he would be the rightful heir to Edenbourg's throne. Dominique had agreed to have the sex of the baby determined, but she'd set up strict conditions.

The physician had sealed the results in an envelope that was now in Josephine's possession. The envelope was to be opened an hour before the coronation of the new king and only in the event that Michael wasn't found.

Although Nicholas was the rightful heir, Josephine didn't want him on the throne until they knew who was responsible for the kidnapping. Until the traitor was found, she felt nobody in her immediate family was safe.

But, she also sensed a danger with Luke becoming king. She didn't trust him, somehow knew that once he sat on the throne there would be no way for her family to reclaim what was rightfully theirs. She knew that if Dominique carried a son, the news of a new heir would rally the people behind her family.

As always, the approach of night deepened the despair, the utter ache in her heart. Would she know if Michael was already dead? Was that why her heart felt so empty, so profoundly grieved?

No, she couldn't lose hope. Isabel had finally confessed what she and Adam Sinclair were trying to do. Although Josephine feared for her daughter, she also clung to the hope that they would be successful, that they would find Michael alive and well.

She had to hang on to that hope. She had to believe that fate wouldn't be so cruel as to open her heart to the love she felt for her husband and not give her a chance to tell him of that love.

Chapter Eight

Two weeks. For two weeks Adam and Isabel had been going to meetings in the bunker with no positive results. They had listened to litany after litany of complaints and proposed changes, but had learned nothing that would lead them to the missing king.

Adam was now stretched out on the bed, a pad and pencil in hand. Isabel was in the bathroom taking a shower. He plumped the pillow behind him, then stared down at the notepad.

On it he'd written a list of potential palace suspects in the kidnapping. The list was dismally short. Edward...Luke...Luke's younger brother, Jake. It still made little sense that any of them would be involved simply to succeed to the throne.

He'd also made a list of names they had learned of people who belonged to the group they had successfully infiltrated. Unfortunately for most of them he only had first names. Nobody used their full name and it would have looked suspicious had they asked.

The few full names he'd managed to get had come from Pam, who continued to try to be a help, but simply didn't possess the information they wanted most.

He stared at the lists of names and tried to ignore the sound of the shower running in the next room, tried to suppress the vivid mental picture of Isabel standing naked beneath a steamy spray of water.

It was after two. Adam had spent the past two hours working on the clean-up in the tavern, and he'd been surprised to find Isabel still awake when he'd returned to the room.

Restless and anxiety-ridden because Luke's coronation was in less than a week, she had finally decided a long, hot shower might help her sleep.

Adam picked up his pencil once again and began to doodle on the paper as the water in the shower stopped running. He frowned. Now she was drying off, sliding a towel across the smooth skin of her shoulders, down her flat abdomen, over those silky, shapely legs.

Over the past three weeks he'd learned her night-time routine. After drying off, she'd smooth on lotion, a light, fragrant lotion that smelled of lanolin and the faint whisper of peaches.

Then she'd spritz a dash of perfume just behind her ears, and it was that combination of lotion and perfume that filled the room each night, driving Adam to the very brink of lunacy.

He was still doodling on the pad when she left the bathroom moments later. Clad in the lavender nightgown and robe, she swept to her side of the bed and sat.

"I'm going to have to color my hair again," she said and reached a hand up to touch a wet, shiny strand. "The red color is starting to wash out."

"Before you do anything so drastic, we need to talk."

She stretched out on her side of the bed facing him. He tried not to notice as her robe gaped open, giving him a perfect view of her silk-clad breasts. "Talk about what?"

Without makeup, the strength of her bold features was evident, providing her a kind of natural beauty that stirred deeply inside Adam. He knew those lush green eyes of hers would haunt him for a long time after their mock marriage was over.

"How long do we continue this, Isabel? How long do we continue living in this hole-in-the-wall, pretending to be people we are not? When do we say it's time to give up?"

Her eyes flashed with fire and her lips compressed for a moment. "When we find my father. When we know who the traitor is. That's when we stop."

"What if we learn nothing in two months, three months...six months?" Adam drew a deep breath, knowing he was about to say something that would probably make her angry. "Isabel, it's possible we'll never find your father, that the people who are keeping him will never trust us enough to tell us where he is."

She sat up facing him. "I don't believe that," she said firmly, then added softly, "I can't believe that."

Adam sighed. He'd watched her for these past weeks, felt the hope that never wavered inside her. He knew all about that kind of undeviating hope. He'd felt it himself for months after his father's plane had disappeared.

At that time, his hope had been for two separate things...hope that his father would be found alive and well, and the hope that there was a logical explanation for his disappearance that had nothing to do with treason.

But, as time had passed, Adam had been forced to face some painful conclusions. When neither his father nor wreckage of the plane had been found, he'd been forced to accept the possibility that his father had done the unimaginable and betrayed the country he once had professed to love.

He worried that Isabel hadn't even begun to entertain alternatives to her father being found safe and sound. She steadfastly refused to think the outcome might not be good. "Isabel, we can't play this game forever. You have to face the possibility that we might never find your father, that you might never know what happened to your father."

"I can't." The strength that had momentarily tautened her features faded away. Her lower lip trembled and her eyes grew impossibly luminous. "Please, Adam, don't try to strip away my hope." She reached out and took one of his hands in hers. "It's all I have and I need it to get through all of this."

He squeezed her hand, unable to force the issue, unwilling to steal away her hope the way his had been taken from him. "I don't want to take away your hope, Isabel. But, eventually we both have to get back to our jobs and our lives."

"I know." She pulled her hand from his and sighed. She pulled her legs up against her chest and wrapped her arms around them, looking far younger than her years. "I just feel like we're so close to getting answers."

"I can't help but think maybe we're wrong to be so focused on the throne as the ultimate goal," Adam said, gazing down at his lists and doodling in frustration. "Maybe it's more personal than that."

"What do you mean?"

"I don't know, maybe the goal of the mastermind is not to gain control of the throne, but rather to punish your father or your family for some reason."

"As king, my father often had to make difficult decisions, decisions that didn't always make everyone happy. But I can't think of anyone working in the palace with my father who might have been that angry with him, and we know the mastermind is in the palace."

"I've been sitting here making lists of names, but no warning bells have jingled in my head," Adam explained.

"Looks like you've been doing more than making lists." She smiled at him. "I didn't realize you were such an artist," she teased and pointed to his doodling.

"It's supposed to be a honeycomb," Adam explained.

She frowned and reached out for the pad. He handed it to her. "What?" he asked.

"This reminds me of something...." Her frown deepened.

"What?" he asked and sat up straight.

She stared at his pad with an intensity that shot adrenaline through him. "What, Isabel? What does it remind you of?" he asked softly.

Her eyes didn't waver from the paper. Seconds

ticked by and suddenly her gaze flew to his. "The catacombs," she exclaimed.

"The catacombs? What catacombs?"

Her eyes were lit with excitement. "My father showed me a picture of them. They're ancient...mostly in ruins...and run beneath the palace." Her hands reached out and grabbed Adam's tightly. "Like honeycombs...they look like honeycombs running beneath the streets. Honeycombs...catacombs...perhaps the clue was in Shane's words after all."

The adrenaline that had begun to soar through Adam now exploded. "How do you get to these catacombs?" he asked, shocked at the very idea of an ancient world beneath the streets.

"The only entryway I know is through the chapel. Behind the altar is a trap door that leads down to them. Adam...do you think he's there? Is it possible that's where they are holding my father?" She half rose from the bed, stopping only because he held tight to her hand. "We have to go...we have to see if he's there."

"Be smart, Isabel, and slow down. We don't know how many people might be guarding him and I'm sure there must be another entrance and exit to these catacombs." He rose from the bed, not releasing his hold on her hand. "We can't go in there unprepared and alone."

She nodded, and he let go of her. "So, what do

we do? I know we need some manpower, but I'm not sure I trust royal security. I don't want the guilty to get word of what we're doing."

"I agree. I've got a squad of men who would give their very lives for King Michael. They're good men, trustworthy and loyal." He looked at his watch. "I can have them ready to move by dawn." He grabbed his jeans and a shirt and headed for the bathroom.

"You aren't doing this without me," Isabel said behind him. As he closed the bathroom door, he heard her grabbing clothes and knew she was dressing for battle...the battle to save her father.

He didn't even consider requesting that she stay here, let him and his men handle the situation. He knew better. There was no way he could keep her out of this. All he could do was hope that he could keep her safe.

The morning sun was just peeking over the horizon when Adam, Isabel and fifteen highly trained navy men descended silently on the chapel on the palace grounds.

Not a word was spoken as they entered the interior of the beautiful place of worship. All the planning, instructions and strategy had been laid out, gone over and solidified in the previous hours.

What Isabel wanted most was to forgo the hours of planning and simply storm the catacombs and find her father. But Isabel had been trained in military matters. She'd been trained by one of the best—Adam.

As she listened to him outline the tactics they would use, her heart swelled with love. He was so smart, so strong and it was obvious, despite the rumors about his father, the men he'd chosen for this particular job admired and respected him.

As they started down the stone stairs revealed by a trap door just behind the chapel altar, Isabel was focused on only one thing…they had to find her father.

She was angry with herself for not thinking about the catacombs before. But the ancient burial grounds had long been forgotten by most of the people of Edenbourg.

As they descended into the depths of the earth, the air turned musty and stale, but the only sound discernible was Isabel's frantically beating heart. It echoed loudly in her ears, making her wonder if it was audible outside of her body.

The men moved like dark shadows soundlessly along the soft rock walls. Isabel knew the catacombs were an intricate network of corridors and rooms and that it might take hours or longer for all of them to be checked.

She was grateful for Adam's presence next to her. His nearness calmed her nerves, focused her energy and eased the tension that was rife inside her.

Would they find her father? Would he be dead or alive? She couldn't imagine spending more than three months in this dark, dank place and was frightened by thoughts of what her father's condition might be if he were found alive.

Flashlights lit their way as they walked further and further away from the entrance and deeper and deeper into the ancient maze.

Here and there the walls were decorated with elaborate frescoes, religious scenes from the Bible painted onto the walls hundreds of years before. It was easy to see where there were actual graves as bricks and slabs of stone depicted final resting places.

With each new crevice or corridor they came upon, several of the men left the group to explore while Adam, Isabel and the rest continued forward.

Finally, they'd gone far enough that Adam and Isabel were alone to proceed along one of the narrow corridors. The flashlight Adam held barely penetrated the black abyss before them.

She fought the need to reach for his hand, knowing he had the flashlight in one and would need his other to be free to reach for his gun. Besides, she'd been trained for battle, trained both physically and mentally. She shouldn't need to hold anyone's hand.

With every step a prayer was on her lips…a prayer to find her father alive. She and her father had battled often because of Isabel rebelling against the role of traditional princess, but those battles were insignificant now. She would gladly adhere to anything her father requested of her in exchange for his health and well-being.

She felt as if they'd walked for hours when she thought she saw a faint illumination in the distance that had nothing to do with Adam's light. She grabbed Adam's arm and pointed. Instantly he clicked off his light.

Ahead, from around a bend in the path, spilled a faint light. Isabel's heart thundered and the hair on the nape of her neck rose. Somebody with a light was just around the corner and she knew it couldn't be any of their group.

Adam gently pushed her behind him as they advanced on the corner. She felt rather than heard the sharp intake of his breath as he peered around, then pressed back against her.

Emotion raced through Isabel at his reaction. Was it her father? Had he seen her father lying dead in this primitive burial ground? She swallowed hard, preparing herself for whatever lay beyond the bend of the wall.

Leaning past Adam, she peered around the corner. Shock riveted through her as she saw Willie

Tammerick seated on a folding chair next to what appeared to be a small room enclosed by bars.

Willie Tammerick...friendly King's Men Tavern patron, perpetual drunk and easygoing riffraff, was apparently not as friendly, drunk or easygoing as he pretended.

Before Adam could stop her, Isabel spun around the corner. "Hey, Willie boy," she said with a lightness of tone that belied the tight constriction of her chest. Willie jumped up, a pistol trained on her. "They told me you were here," she bluffed.

He seemed to relax a little. He sat back down, but didn't lower the gun. "I figured eventually I'd see you down here, you being family to Shane and all."

Isabel pointed to the bars across the entry of a tiny chamber. "Is he in there?" Willie nodded and heart pounding, Isabel stepped up to the bars and peered into the small area lit only with two torches.

Her father sat on a narrow cot. Her heart fell to her toes. In his eyes was no flicker of recognition as he gazed at his eldest daughter.

"He don't look so much like a high-and-mighty king now, does he?" She forced a light tone to her voice. In truth, he looked horrid. He was filthy and his face held the gray pallor of unhealthiness. She had to fight not to jerk open the barred door and rush to his side.

All she wanted was for Willie to relax his guard

enough to lower the gun. She knew the moment that happened, Adam would be around that corner like a bullet shot out of a gun, ready to take Willie down and free the king.

"Does he talk?" she asked.

"Not much." He narrowed his gaze in speculation. "Who told you about this?"

Isabel blanched, unsure how to bluff an answer. Knowing she had mere seconds before Willie would be on to her, she leapt at him.

She hit him square in the chest, toppling him and the chair over as she grabbed the barrel of the gun to keep him from firing at her.

"Isabel!" Her father roared and she was vaguely aware of the sound of him throwing his body against the bars.

At the same time Adam joined the struggle. He kicked the gun from Willie's hand and sent it skittering across the ground.

"Get up, Willie," Adam demanded, his own gun pointed at the man.

Willie slowly got to his feet. "So, who the hell are you?" he asked Adam, not a hint of blurry-eyed drunkenness in his eyes.

"Lieutenant Commander Adam Sinclair, and we've come to free the king."

"Father," Isabel exclaimed, tears welling in her eyes as she grabbed his hands through the bars.

"Unlock the door, Willie," Adam said. Willie didn't move.

"Come on, Willie. It's all over. The game is done and you lost."

"Ah hell, I knew it was probably done when Shane got himself popped." He grabbed the keys that dangled from his belt loop and, still in the line of Adam's gun, moved to the barred door.

The moment he'd unlocked it, Isabel shoved him aside and reached for her father. As her father's arms enclosed her, something broke loose inside her and months of fear and grief exploded in a cascade of tears.

"Are you all right?" she sobbed against his chest. "We've been so worried." She looked up at him and placed a hand on either side of his face. "We heard you had a stroke."

"I did...but I'm all right now." He placed his hands over hers. "My darling daughter, I was so afraid I'd never see you again, never get the opportunity to tell you how proud I am of you...how very much I love you."

Isabel clung to him more tightly, amazed by his words. Her father had never been a very demonstrative man, and he'd certainly never been one for words of love.

At that moment they were joined by some of the other navy men, and Willie was patted down, then handcuffed. "What now?" Isabel asked as she remained in her father's embrace.

"What do you mean, what now?" Michael drew himself up to his full height and released his hold on Isabel. "We put this man in prison and I go back to the palace."

"Begging your pardon, Your Majesty, but I don't think that's a wise idea," Adam said. "There is a traitor in the palace."

"Who?" Michael bellowed with regal force.

"We don't know who, Father," Isabel replied, then looked at Willie. "But, you know, don't you, Willie? You have to be getting your orders from somebody. Tell us who."

Willie shook his head. "I can't."

"I'll make him talk, just give me five minutes alone with him," one of the navy men muttered audibly.

Willie shrugged. "You can beat me, put me on a rack, throw me in prison, do whatever you want to, but I can't give you a name because I don't have the name. Only Shane knew the insider."

"Then how do you get your orders?" Isabel asked.

"I make a phone call," Willie replied. "It's a cell phone number and the man on the other end of that phone tells me what to do."

Isabel looked at Adam, his features looking hard

and dangerous in the dim light. "The first thing we need to do is get my father to his doctor."

"I want to see Josephine," Michael said.

"I don't think it's in your best interest to return to the palace." Adam frowned, obviously thinking of alternatives. "I have a place, a little cottage in the country. We'll take you there until we can decide what our next move should be."

His words reminded Isabel that this was not over yet. Although they had found her father, until the mastermind behind the kidnapping was found, neither the king nor Nicholas was safe.

"Isabel, you go get your mother," Adam instructed her, then turned his attention to a young military man. "Green...you know where my off-base place is, don't you?"

"Yes, sir," the man replied.

"You go with Isabel. Bring the queen to my cottage." He looked at two more of his men. "Simpson and Keller, I'm placing our prisoner under your guard. Bring him to my place as well. We'll figure out exactly what to do once we're there."

Isabel hugged her father one last time then with Ensign Green she left the catacombs.

It was nearly two hours later that Ensign Green pulled up in front of a small, attractive cottage. Isabel and her mother sat in the back seat of his car holding hands.

Nobody except the soldiers who had been there

and now Josephine knew that the king had been found alive and well. Before Ensign Green could turn off the car engine, Josephine was out of the car and running for the front door.

Isabel hurried after her mother and caught up with her in the living room, where Isabel watched as her father and mother flew into one another's arms.

In the time since she'd seen her father, he'd obviously showered and shaved, although his hair remained unusually long and his face was still pale and drawn.

"Michael...my love," Josephine cried, tears trekking down her cheeks as she clung to her husband.

"Josephine...my Josephine," Michael replied.

Isabel watched the two in wonder. She'd never before seen her parents hug...kiss. Although she'd always seen them treat each other with respect and admiration, she'd never seen them express such unabashed love for one another.

"Isabel." Adam called her name softly and gestured toward the front door.

She nodded and together they stepped outside, giving the king and his queen some precious time alone.

They walked several paces away from the house, the air balmy and filled with the scent of green pastures and sweet flowers. "How long have you had this place?" she asked.

He stopped and leaned against the side of Ensign Green's car. "I bought it a couple of weeks after my father's plane went down." He stared at the cottage for a long moment, then turned and looked at her. "When the rumors started, I thought I might need to build a civilian life for myself."

"Why?" she asked in surprise. "If your father was a traitor, it is his crime, not yours."

"But if the rumors persist and if even one of my men doubts me, then I'll leave my post." His eyes were dark...haunted. "I can't be a leader if there are any doubts about my integrity."

She wished desperately she had some answers for him, wished she'd heard something positive from the investigators she'd put on the case of the missing prototype. But, there had been no word.

"Can you believe Willie Tammerick was in on this all along?" she asked, changing the subject. "And he tried to push us toward the Patriots, knowing all along he was one of the guilty ones."

Adam shook his head. "He fooled me completely. I thought Blake Hariman and his group were the guilty ones, but I guess they're just another bunch of disillusioned rebels."

"Where is Willie now?"

"In one of the bedrooms with two guards. Your father and I have come up with a plan."

"What kind of plan?" she asked.

Quickly, he outlined what they intended to do. As she listened she tried not to focus on how handsome he looked with the moonlight on his strong features.

Her mind exploded with a vision of her mother and father in one another's arms, the love that had filled the room when they'd kissed. She wanted that…she wanted that with Adam. She wanted the "marriage" she'd shared with him over the past three weeks to be real.

She wanted to awaken each morning in his arms, go to sleep after making love with him each night. She wanted to build a life with him, a life of dreams and hopes, of laughter and passion.

Her heart was heavy as she realized the truth of the situation. In finding her father, they'd brought to an end any personal relationship they might have shared. She'd regained her father, and in the process had to relinquish the man that she loved.

"We have much to talk about," Michael said to his wife. He smoothed a hand down her cheek, his eyes holding an expression of love she'd never seen there before. "I've had lots of time to think."

"As I have," she replied. "I love you, Michael, and I've been so afraid I wouldn't get a chance to tell you how very much I love you."

His lips captured hers in a fiery kiss that spoke

of a depth of abiding love and passion she'd never tasted in his kisses before. "No more separate lives," he said as the kiss ended. "Things are going to change. I want you...need you by my side every minute of the day for the rest of my life."

Josephine's heart expanded with a happiness she'd never known before. This man...this king was her husband...the love of her life. "And I want to be at your side for every minute for the rest of our lives."

Michael's blue eyes deepened in hue. "But, before we can do anything else, we must find out who is behind all this. We have to find the traitor."

Josephine nodded. She could face anything, do anything as long as she had Michael by her side.

Chapter Nine

"What do you want me to do with that?" Willie asked as he stared at the phone Adam had just shoved in front of him.

They had moved Willie into the living area of the small cottage. The two men guarding him, Adam, Isabel, Queen Josephine and King Michael stood in a circle around the man.

"I want you to call your boss and tell him the king is dead."

Isabel heard her mother's sharp intake of breath and watched as Josephine reached for her husband's hand. Isabel had never seen her mother look so vulnerable and she knew it was love for Isabel's father that made her vulnerable.

"And what do I get out of doing such a thing?" Willie asked.

"I will spare your life," King Michael said softly.

Willie hesitated a long moment, then nodded and picked up the phone. "Yeah, it's me," he said to whoever had answered the phone. "The bee is dead." Another pause. "Hell yes, I'm sure. Must have been a massive stroke that got him." He listened another moment longer. "Okay, I'll take care of it." He hung up.

"What did he say?" Isabel asked.

"He told me to get rid of the body."

A shiver worked its way up Isabel's spine at the cold words. How easily it could have been that her father might have died and nobody would have ever found his body.

"We'll take him to the naval base and lock him up there until all this is over," Adam said. "With the betrayer now thinking that both King Michael and Prince Nicholas are dead, we're hoping a move will be made that will reveal his identity."

King Michael held his hand out to Adam. "I appreciate all you've done, Lieutenant Commander, and I appreciate the use of your home until the coronation on Saturday."

Adam nodded.

"If you're staying here, then so am I," Josephine said to her husband.

The look Michael gave his wife sent a different kind of shiver through Isabel, a shiver of wistfulness, and a desire to someday have a man look at her in that same way.

"For tonight, you stay," he said softly. "But, tomorrow you must return to the palace and pretend that everything is as it was. It's important that nobody know anything has changed. As far as everyone else is concerned I am still missing and Nicholas is still presumed to be dead."

It took nearly an hour to get Willie and a couple of Adam's men dispatched back to the base. Two men were assigned to stay at the cottage for the protection of the king and queen.

With everything arranged, Adam and Isabel left the cottage. Although Isabel was overjoyed by the return of her father, her heart was heavy as she realized her time with Adam had come to an end.

"I don't want you going back to the King's Men Tavern," he said as they walked to his car. "The group will know that not only is the bee gone, but his keeper as well. It will be dangerous for either of us to show ourselves again."

She forced a light smile. "I sure hate to give up all those awesome clothes."

He smiled. "You're back to being a princess, and those aren't the clothes for a princess to wear."

She nodded and together they got into his car. He would drive her back to the palace, where she would resume living in her luxury quarters. He was taking her home, but that's not how it felt.

Home was that tiny room on the third floor of the bar, where she and Adam had slept together on a lumpy, soft bed for the past couple of weeks. Home was in their laughter, in the kisses they had shared.

But she knew he didn't feel the same depth of love for her. He couldn't and walk away from her. She only hoped she had the strength to walk away from him without making an utter fool of herself.

"While you were getting your mother, I had a local physician I trust check out your father," Adam said, breaking the silence that had built between them.

"What did he say?"

"Of course without the proper equipment of a hospital, he couldn't be certain as to what extent your father's stroke caused damage, but because there are no outward lingering effects, he felt confident that it was a fairly mild stroke."

"Father needs to see his own doctor."

"He wants to wait until after the coronation on Saturday. We're hoping the guilty party will reveal himself before then and King Michael trusts nobody at this time, not even the royal physician."

Isabel sighed. "How sad, to be unable to trust the people around you."

"Where there is power and position to be gained, there are always people who want to either steal it from you or share it with you."

How well Isabel understood this. "I often wonder if Sebastian would be so eager to marry me if I were simply a woman and not a princess."

Adam turned and cast her a quick, meaningful look. "But, it's impossible for you to separate the two. You are a woman, but you'll also always be a princess."

Her heart fell a little further in her chest at his words. She knew what he was subtly telling her was that as a princess, there was no hope for the two of them.

"Did he tell you about the actual kidnapping?" she asked, trying to stay focused on her father and not on the painful shattering of her heart.

"According to your father, on the morning of LeAnn's christening, he received a phone call from Edward telling him that Edward and his sons were in Edenbourg. Edward asked your father to meet him in private."

"So it was Uncle Edward all along," Isabel exclaimed.

"I don't think so," Adam countered. "Your father now doesn't believe it was Edward that he spoke to."

"But, it had to have been somebody who knew that Edward and his sons had come to Edenbourg." She sighed again, finding the entire thing far too exhausting. "It's all so confusing."

Again she thought of those first moments between her mother and father and the words of love her father had spoken to Isabel. "He's changed. Somehow these months in captivity have changed my father."

"That's not surprising. You can't face the possibility of your own death without it affecting you."

As the palace appeared in the distance, a hollow ache throbbed in her chest. She fought against it, but the ache spread, filling her with a dismal feeling of loss.

It was crazy to feel as if she'd lost what she'd never really had, crazy to grieve the loss of a marriage that had only been pretend.

When they reached the gates of the palace, Adam was waved through. He parked before the compound where Isabel's private quarters were located.

When he shut off the engine, she felt his gaze on her, and as she turned to look at him, to her horror, tears filled her eyes. "I know it sounds stupid, but I feel like we're getting a divorce." A divorce she didn't want, she thought as the tears spilled down her cheeks.

He reached over and touched her arm. It was a light, easy touch, but sweet sensations soared through her at the contact. "Come on, I'll walk you to the door."

Together they got out of the car and he fell into step beside her as they approached the building. There were so many things she wanted to say, but her emotions were lodged in the back of her throat, making speech momentarily impossible.

"Isabel," he began, his voice gentle. "Part of the danger of undercover operations is that sometimes people get caught up in the roles they are playing, the fantasy they are spinning."

She nodded, unable to do anything else as they stopped just short of the door where two royal guards stood sentry.

"It's time to put the game behind us," he continued, his eyes dark and fathomless. "The operation was a success and now its time for you to put your hair back to its normal color and wipe the make-up off your face."

His hand reached up and gently touched her cheek and once again Isabel's vision blurred with tears. She knew in her heart that it would be the last, gentle, personal touch she received from him.

The next time she saw him he would once again be Lieutenant Commander Adam Sinclair and she would be Princess Isabel, a cabinet member and in the Ministry of Defense. There would be no more personal talk, no more sharing of dreams or lives.

He dropped his hand. "It's time for you to resume your station as Princess of Edenbourg, with all the duties and responsibilities that go along with the title."

He stood so close to her, and she fought the impulse to lean forward and raise her lips for one last kiss. She was afraid that if she raised her lips to his, he wouldn't kiss her and her heart would certainly shatter into a million pieces.

"I'll see you at the coronation, Your Highness," he said, then saluted her and turned to walk back to his car.

He'd taken only a couple of steps when she softly called his name. He turned back to look at her, his eyes dark and unreadable.

"I just want you to know that I loved being your wife," she said.

He paused, then nodded. Without saying anything, he once again rotated on his heels and headed for his car.

Isabel watched as he started his engine, then pulled away. As his car disappeared from her view, the hollow ache that had been in her heart expanded.

She'd told him she loved being his wife, and that was as close as she could come to telling him she loved him. But, he hadn't even told her he'd liked being her husband.

It was over. Truly over. Their covert operation had been a huge success, and the only price she'd had to pay was the ache of a broken heart.

The most difficult thing Adam had ever done in his life was to walk away from Isabel without taking her in his arms, indulging in one final kiss.

For the past weeks that they had spent living as man and wife Adam had told himself that what he felt for her was nothing more than lust...a mere physical desire.

But he knew now he'd only been fooling himself. Yes, he wanted Isabel. He wanted to taste the sweetness of her lips, make love to her over and over again, but he wanted that because he loved her.

He loved her irritating little habits, the inner strength she possessed, and the soft vulnerability he'd been surprised to find in her. He loved Princess Isabel and he intended to do nothing about it.

He had nothing to offer her. A name besmirched by scandal and not a drop of blue blood inside him. He had to put her out of his mind and out of his heart. Eventually she would please the country and her father by marrying Sebastian Lansbury or some other man with political connections and wealth.

In two days Luke's coronation was scheduled to occur and before the ceremony, King Michael would appear to resume his rightful place on the throne. After that, Adam would return to the task of trying to solve the mystery of the disappearance of the Phantom and attempt to clear his father's name.

He had the sickening feeling that his attempt to prove his father's innocence fell into the same category as his love for Princess Isabel. Utterly hopeless.

* * *

The next two days passed swiftly. Adam spent much of his time in his cottage with King Michael, Prince Nicholas, Marcus Kent, the king's High Counsel, and Lieutenant Ben Lockhart. The five men, along with a handful of trusted naval personnel had worked out a plan of action to get King Michael back on the throne.

Although they had hoped that telling the mastermind that King Michael was dead might force an action that would reveal the guilty, that hadn't happened. However, King Michael had agreed that whether the guilty party revealed himself or not, he had to reclaim his position before Luke could officially be crowned king.

With this in mind, the night before the coronation, King Michael and Prince Nicholas were moved to a secret place in the palace and Adam found himself alone in his cottage.

He'd always found this little isolated house a peaceful haven. But, on this night, the silence crashed around him, giving him far too much time to think…and his thoughts, as always, were of Isabel.

It had only been two days since they'd stopped their game of husband and wife. But he missed her. He missed her crankiness in the mornings, that first full smile of the day that exploded over her features and reverberated in his heart.

He missed the scent of her, that whisper of spice and flowers that stirred something deep inside him. He missed her laughter, her strong will and yes, even her stubbornness.

But he was not for her, he reminded himself yet again as he popped the tab on a beer and eased down on the sofa to relax.

Tomorrow would prove an unforgettable day in Edenbourg. Adam knew the majority of the country adored King Michael and his family and many had not been looking forward to Luke Stanbury, a young man not even raised in their country, assuming the title.

He sat up as he spied headlights beaming across the front of his cottage. Very few people knew of this place. Who could be coming to see him?

Curious, he stood and went to the front window, stunned to see Isabel getting out of her car.

"Princess Isabel, what are you doing here?" he asked as he opened the door to admit her.

"Adam, we need to talk," she exclaimed.

He pointed her toward the sofa, unsure he wanted to hear what she had to say. He knew she fancied herself in love with him, but also knew there was absolutely no future for them. He didn't want a difficult scene with her, was afraid of himself and his own emotions where she was concerned.

He felt thankful that she was clad in a sedate dress that fell to just below her knees. "I see you've got your own hair color back,'' he observed as he sat in a chair across from her perch on the sofa.

''Yes.'' She raked a hand through her hair, then leaned forward, her eyes so intense he found it difficult to meet her gaze. ''Adam, I have news for you.''

''News?'' He looked at her curiously. ''What kind of news?''

''About your father.''

The words plowed into Adam's chest, creating an instant tightness of wariness and anxiety. ''How did you get news?'' His voice sounded distant...far away to his own ears.

''When I called you back here to help investigate my father's kidnapping, I assigned several investigators to continue seeking answers to your father's disappearance.''

''And what did they find?'' His chest ached and he realized he didn't even know what he wanted the answers to be.

If his father was dead, and the whole thing had been a tragic accident, then Adam had his good name back, but his father was dead forever. And if his father was a traitor and had flown that plane to another country, then Adam would forever live beneath the shadow of that treachery, but at least he'd know his father was still alive someplace in the world.

''They found the plane, Adam.''

"Where?" The word eased from him in a half breath.

"Off the coast of Sweden, almost buried in the floor of the sea."

Instantly he understood the implication of her words. His father was dead. He gazed down at the floor and fought against the deep sorrow that ripped through him with this final knowledge. He'd thought he'd been prepared for whatever they might eventually learn, but the pierce of mourning caught him off guard.

"They managed to bring up a portion of the plane, enough to determine that mechanical failure was the reason they were so far off course and was the determining cause of the accident."

He sensed, rather than saw her approach him. She sat on the floor at his feet and took his hands in both of hers, forcing him to look at her.

Her eyes were the softest green he'd ever seen and he saw the love that resided there...love and compassion for him. He wasn't sure what hurt more, the ache of his father's death, or the ache of knowing she loved him and he would never do anything about it.

"He died a hero, Adam," she said softly. "Your father and those two pilots died in the line of duty, for the country that they loved."

For a year, turmoil had bubbled inside Adam and now the emotion he'd kept stuffed so firmly threatened to explode outward. He was going to lose it, but he didn't want to do that in front of Isabel.

He stood and quickly pulled her to her feet. He needed to get her out before he lost control. He needed time alone…time to grieve for the father he knew now without question was lost forever.

He saw the surprise in her eyes as he led her to the door…surprise and a touch of pain as she realized he was about to ask her to go. "Isabel," he said softly. "You have brought me the gift of the truth, but it's a double-edged sword and I need some time alone to assimilate it all."

"I know you're in pain right now, but I wish you'd let me comfort you." Those eyes of her were so filled with love. "Adam, I…"

He placed a fingertip across her lips. "Don't say it, Isabel." He knew she was about to tell him that she loved him and he couldn't stand to hear those words spoken aloud. Not now. Not ever.

"Thank you, Isabel. Now go home and I'll see you tomorrow at the coronation."

She turned to leave, but he stopped her as she stepped off the porch. "Isabel…I liked being married to you, too." He said, then closed the door.

He leaned heavily against the door and felt the sting of tears. As he closed his eyes, the tears seeped down his cheeks and he didn't know if he was crying for the father he had lost…or the woman he would never have.

Chapter Ten

Isabel couldn't remember the last time she had seen the Edenbourg Cathedral so filled with people. Not only were dignitaries, family members and high-ranking people from Edenbourg present, but the coronation of Luke had also brought a wave of people from the small countries of Wynborough and Thortonburg.

Besides the royalty and prominent visitors, it appeared that most of the country of Edenbourg had turned out for the celebration. Outside the cathedral, throngs of people crowded the streets. Children rode their fathers' shoulders in an effort to get a peek at the new king. Women wore flowers in their hair and carried bouquets in their arms in tribute to the day.

But, what warmed Isabel's heart the most were the many signs and posters she saw with her father's picture on them. Although she knew nobody would overtly rebel against the new king, the people were silently showing where their hearts were…with the missing king and his supposedly dead son.

As people continued to be seated in the cathedral, Isabel scanned the crowd for one particular familiar face. Adam's. Her heart ached for him. She had never known that heartache could hurt so much.

She'd hoped when she'd gone to his cottage the night before with the news about his father that he would throw his arms around her and finally admit his love for her.

She'd hoped the stain on his father's name had been the barrier that had kept him from proclaiming his love. But, apparently, having closure about his father hadn't been enough.

She shifted on her chair, hoping she could get through the day without crying. She'd always believed herself to be a strong woman, but loving Adam had made her feel uncharacteristically weak.

"Are you all right?" Queen Josephine's green eyes met Isabel's.

"Of course, I'm fine," Isabel replied without hesitation. She wasn't about to do or say anything to ruin the glow of happiness in her mother's green eyes.

Isabel couldn't remember the last time she'd seen her mother look so beautiful. She looked elegant and dignified, but also feminine and happy. It was love, Isabel knew, that gave her that special, wonderful radiance.

Isabel and the members of King Michael's family were seated all together in a little balcony to the right of the raised platform of the altar. There, Luke sat next to his father, along with the clergy and people who would officiate at the coronation ceremony.

Edward's appearance shocked Isabel. She hadn't seen him since she'd gone undercover and his physical deterioration was appalling. He'd lost a lot of weight and looked beyond haggard.

Isabel looked at the men and women surrounding Luke…men and women in high position. Somebody in this cathedral was the traitor who had kidnapped her father and tried to kidnap her brother. Somebody in this cathedral had, without hesitation or conscience, told Willie to get rid of her father's body as if it were nothing more than a piece of unwanted garbage.

Who? She scanned the people who had been closest to her father. Who could be responsible for such a terrible thing?

The priest had just stood to begin the ceremony when a murmur began near the front door. The murmuring built, growing louder, and as the door to the cathedral opened, Isabel could hear the roar of the crowd outside.

Her heart tightened in anticipation as she heard what was being chanted. "King Michael. King Michael."

At that moment, her father and her brother strode up the aisle, followed closely by Lieutenant Commander Adam Sinclair, Marcus Kent and Lieutenant Benjamin Lockhart.

Adam…Adam, Isabel's heart cried out. He looked so handsome, resplendent in his crisp uniform. Her love for him ached deep inside her, and she knew no man would ever touch her heart as he had.

When the men got about halfway to the altar area, a silence descended. It was obvious Edward, Luke and the officiating clergy couldn't tell what was going on. Luke stood, and the moment he saw King Michael and Prince Nicholas, his pleasant smile fell away and rage contorted his features.

"No!" His voice seemed to shake the very rafters of the building. "He told me you were dead! You are supposed to be dead!"

A collective gasp filled the church.

"Guards, arrest that man." King Michael's voice rang out with strength and authority as he pointed to Luke. "Take him into the chancery."

"My God, Luke, what have you done?" Edward's voice was audible just before the crowd went wild.

As the men disappeared into the nearby office, Isabel, her mother and the rest of her family hurriedly followed. Isabel's heart thudded in horror. Luke. It had been Luke all along.

When they entered the office, Luke was seated next to his father, and Adam stood before him.

"You were the one who made that phone call to King Michael on the day of LeAnn's christening. You pretended to be your father, didn't you?" Adam asked, his gray eyes like tumultuous storms. "You arranged all of it. You've been pulling strings behind the scenes for months."

"Tell him he's wrong, son," Edward said softly. "There has to be a mistake here." He looked beseechingly at Adam, then at his brother, Isabel's father. "Michael, there has to be a mistake."

King Michael eyed his brother with compassion. "The mistake was in the words he uttered the moment he saw me. Only one man had word of my death…the mastermind behind the kidnapping."

"But why?" Edward's heartache was palpable. "Is this so, Luke? Why would you do such a thing?"

"Why?" Luke laughed, a bitter sound that sent chills up Isabel's spine. His blue eyes glittered cold as ice as he glared at his father. "If you hadn't been such a stupid fool years ago and moved to the States, then we might have lived as royalty.''

Gone was the affection that had always lit his eyes when he spoke to his father, and in its place was a raging animosity. ''The Edenbourg Stanburys had it all…and we had nothing.''

His gaze swept over Isabel's family. ''I came here a year ago to visit. But, your guards wouldn't even let me in and none of my phone calls were put through. They thought I was lying about being related to the precious royal family.''

Now that he'd begun speaking, it was as if a dam had burst inside him. ''I spent a little time in the King's Men Tavern and met Shane Moore and I made some plans to take back what should have been mine.''

''So, you set up your brother. You made sure Jake would happen upon the crash and become a suspect in King Michael's disappearance,'' Adam said, obviously putting together all the pieces of Luke's demented puzzle.

''Good old Jake was supposed to be my fall guy,'' Luke said, and with each word his father seemed to slump farther and farther down in his chair. ''I requested a copy of the Edenbourg Treatise using Jake's stationery and even forged Jake's signature to add to the evidence pointing towards Jake.''

''But…I don't understand.'' King Michael

frowned. "If you kidnapped me and kidnapped Nicholas, you still wouldn't sit on the throne. How were you to know your father would become ill?"

The sly grin that curved Luke's mouth made Isabel's skin feel as if insects were walking on it. "Father loves his cup of tea in the evenings," he said. "And I never neglected to fix it for him."

"You've been poisoning him!" Isabel blurted out.

"My God," Edward gasped. "Was it so important that you rule Edenbourg?"

Luke snorted derisively, his eyes wild with madness. "I don't care about ruling this stupid little country," he exclaimed.

"Then why? What has this all been about?" Adam asked.

"The Chamber of Riches. Once I was king and had all the treasure, then I didn't care what Shane Moore and his band of men did with this country. I just wanted the wealth...all the treasure."

He looked at King Michael. "You were kidnapped so I could gain the location and password or whatever to get into the Chamber of Riches. It was Willie Tammerick's job to get you to tell him. Then you had your stroke and couldn't...or wouldn't talk. So, we kidnapped Nicholas. But, of course we actually got Ben Lockhart, who couldn't tell us anything about the Chamber of Riches."

His gaze slid to Dominique. "When I realized

she might carry a new heir, I had to hurry things up a bit to get my father off the throne and me sitting in it.''

"Get him out of here," Edward cried weakly. "I can't stand the sight of him. My own flesh and blood would have killed me for money."

"Take him away," King Michael told the guards. "And see to it that my brother gets immediate medical attention."

It was a half hour more before Michael and Josephine stood in front of the crowd in the cathedral, his arms raised as the crowd chanted his name over and over again.

Isabel's gaze went to Adam, who stood just to the right of her father and her brother. As if he felt her looking at him, he returned the gaze and she knew he shared her joy that the guilty party had been found out and would now spend years behind bars.

She also knew that as her father addressed the people, soldiers were on their way to pick up members of the group that had held King Michael. All the intrigue, all the danger to her family was over. Beneath the joy that danced in her heart was her ever-present love for Adam.

"My people," King Michael began as the roar of the crowd finally subsided. "It has been far too long since I stood before you." The crowd once again went wild and King Michael raised his hands for silence. "And in my time of captivity and isolation, I've had much time to reflect on what is important in my life. When everything else had been stripped from me, I realized what was left was love...love for this country and love for my family."

He reached for Queen Josephine's hand. "I'd like time to spend with my wife...my children and grandchildren." He smiled at Dominique. "And I understand Edenbourg will welcome a new princess in the future."

Cheers went up and tears of happiness filled Isabel's eyes as she realized she would have a new niece to love and cherish.

"You came for a coronation," King Michael continued, "and we're going to have a coronation. I'd like nothing better than to see my son seated on the throne. I know he will rule with justice and compassion."

"Long live King Nicholas." The crowd roared.

A new wave of tears burned at Isabel's eyes as she watched the ceremony that would make her brother king. She recognized that a new era was being born right before her eyes. Her father was making a choice of love over duty and again Isabel's thoughts turned to Adam.

She couldn't find him in the crowd and didn't see him again until they left the cathedral and traveled to the grand ballroom in the palace for a celebration party.

The ballroom was crowded as Isabel walked in. The mood was joyous and everyone seemed to be smiling or laughing…everyone except Isabel. It was difficult to laugh with a broken heart.

She wandered the room aimlessly, finally stopping near where King Nicholas sat receiving tributes from well-wishers. She frowned as she saw Sebastian Lansbury approaching her. His blond hair gleamed in the light from the dozens of chandeliers and a smooth, practiced smile curved his lips.

"Isabel, my dear. I've been frantic for weeks, ever since your secretary told me you'd gone into seclusion." His blue eyes seemed to be peering just over her left shoulder and Isabel realized he was looking at his own reflection in the shining marble just behind her.

"Yes, I sneaked away for a couple of weeks with my lover," she replied flippantly.

That got his attention. His gaze shot to her face. "Excuse me?"

Isabel felt the rise of a blush warm her face. What was she doing? Why had she said that? "Sebastian, I'm sure you are probably a very nice man, but I'd really rather be alone right now."

At that moment she spied Adam standing alone near a doorway that led out onto a veranda. "Surely you don't mean that," Sebastian said with a small laugh. "They are getting ready to start the dancing. Wouldn't you like to dance with me?"

"Sebastian, go find another woman to dance with. I don't feel like dancing and I'm never, ever going to marry you." In fact, she was trying desperately not to cry. Now that all the drama was over, her father and brother were safe and there was absolutely nothing more to occupy her thoughts, the pain in her heart seemed overwhelming.

She breathed a sigh of relief as Sebastian wandered off. She looked over to where Adam stood talking to her brother. Perhaps she would never marry. She couldn't imagine herself with any other man.

"You're in love with him."

Isabel turned to see Nicholas's wife, Rebecca, standing next to her. "Who, Sebastian?"

Rebecca wrinkled her nose. "No, I know you have better taste than that. I'm talking about Adam."

Isabel considered telling a fib, but she couldn't. Her mouth couldn't form a falsehood where her love for Adam was concerned. "Yes," she finally said softly.

"And he loves you," Rebecca said. "He looks at you just like Nicholas looks at me, as if you are his world."

Isabel stared at Rebecca, wondering if it were

possible. "You really think so...you think he loves me?"

Rebecca smiled. "I know he does." She took Isabel's hand in hers. "And if you are smart, you'll follow your heart, and you won't let him get away."

Tears rose to Isabel's eyes and she squeezed Rebecca's hand. "You are going to be a wonderful queen for the country."

Rebecca smiled and released Isabel's hand as the orchestra began to play. "As long as my main job is loving the king, I'll be all right."

"You'd better go. Nobody will dance until you and Nicholas do."

A moment later Isabel watched as King Nicholas and Queen Rebecca took the center of the ballroom floor. As they danced their eyes were for one another alone.

Was Rebecca right? Did Adam love her? Or, was Rebecca so deeply in love with Nicholas she saw love where there was none?

Isabel once again looked at Adam only to find his gaze locked on hers. In a single split second of their eye contact, she saw his love shining there and she knew there was only one thing to do...follow her heart.

Adam had watched Isabel talking with Sebastian Lansbury and he'd been shocked at the wave of jealousy that tore through him. On some level he recognized that they made an attractive couple…Lansbury with his cool blond looks and Isabel with her smoldering dark sensuality.

He tried not to remember how she'd felt in his arms on the mornings when they'd awakened with their bodies tangled together. He didn't want to remember the passion…the desire in the kisses they'd shared, the white heat of want that had marked their days and nights together.

And he sure as heck didn't want to think about how difficult it was going to be to work with her and not remember the intimacy they'd shared in their pretend marriage.

What he needed to do was get out of here, go someplace where he wouldn't catch sight of her, wouldn't have to watch her talking to, perhaps dancing with, Sebastian Lansbury.

He'd just about made it to the door of the ballroom when she materialized in front of him. She looked like a burst of spring in the emerald dress that perfectly matched her eyes. And instantly he could smell the sweet fragrance of her, the scent that shot a wave of longing through him.

"Lieutenant Commander Sinclair," she said in greeting.

"Your Highness." He bowed, stiffly formal and suddenly on edge. She had that look in her eyes...the excited, agitated look that always spelled trouble.

"It's been a wonderful day, hasn't it?" she asked.

He nodded. "It's always nice when there's a happy ending."

Her gaze held his for a long moment. "Would you dance with me, Adam?"

He wanted to say no. He didn't want to put himself through the ordeal of one last opportunity to hold her close, to feel her warmth against him, to look into those lovely eyes.

He wanted to say no. But he couldn't.

With resignation, he took her in his arms and together they moved across the dance floor to the slow rhythm of the music.

For Adam it was heaven, to have her in his arms once again. As always, he marveled at how neatly their bodies fit together, how absolutely right she felt next to him.

They had danced for only a few moments when she tilted her head back to look at him. "I've missed you, Adam," she said softly.

"Don't, Isabel," he replied painfully.

"Don't what? Don't tell you I missed you? Don't tell you I love you? If I don't tell you, I might explode."

"Isabel, you are a princess," he protested, her words piercing him right to his very soul.

"I am," she agreed solemnly. "And you are the man I want to spend the rest of my life with."

"I have nothing to give you."

She smiled, that beautiful smile that swept warmth across him, through him. "If you give me your love, then it's enough."

How easy it would be to fall into her words, to drown in the sweet light of her eyes. How easy it would be to follow his desire, his heart, knowing the path would lead him to her.

"It's not as simple as that," he said.

"But it is. If you love me as much as I love you, then it really is that simple. Tell me, Adam. Do you love me?" She caught her lower lip in her teeth, her body vibrating with tension.

He wished he could lie. It would be so much easier on them both if he could simply tell her he didn't love her. But he couldn't form the words to deny what was in his heart. His mouth positively refused to negate his love for her.

"I do," the words slipped out with a sigh. "I do love you, Isabel." Once begun, his confession continued to seep out of him. "I loved you when you were a raw recruit under my command. I loved you when you left my command and took the position in the Ministry of Defense. There are days I feel as if I have spent a lifetime loving you."

With each word he spoke the sparkle in her eyes grew brighter until they were impossibly lit. "But,

Isabel...that doesn't change who you are...who I am. You must adhere to your father's wishes, and now the wishes of your brother.''

Isabel nodded. "You're right." She stopped dancing and grabbed his hand. "Come with me," she said and began to tug him toward the raised platform where King Nicholas and Queen Rebecca and King Michael and Queen Josephine were seated.

"What are you doing?" he asked, vaguely aware that Isabel's entire family were on or around the platform.

He saw Marcus Kent with his arm around the very pregnant Princess Dominique. Jake Stanbury was talking to his wife, Rowena, their love for one another apparent in their body language. Ben Lockhart and Meagan Moore were also nearby and Adam knew it wouldn't be long before the two of them were happily married.

The king's kidnapping had accomplished one thing, it had made the people close to the king find love...just as Adam had found love with Isabel. But Adam was simply an officer in the Royal Edenbourg Navy, not the kind of stuff King Michael would want for his daughter, not the kind of royal blood King Nicholas would want for his sister.

"Just stand right here," Isabel said as they stopped just in front of the platform. She released his hold on her hand and he watched curiously as she stepped forward, plucked a flower from one of the nearby lavish arrangements, then returned to where Adam stood.

"What are you doing?" he asked under his breath, aware that the music had stopped and she had drawn the attention of the people in the ballroom.

"This is an ancient custom," she explained. She kissed the flower, then tucked it behind Adam's ear. Adam looked at her in confusion, only to see her watching her father and brother.

He followed her gaze, and watched as first King Nicholas, then King Michael nodded and smiled. The crowded ballroom erupted in cheers.

"What's going on?" he asked in bewilderment.

Isabel smiled. "My father and the new King of Edenbourg have just blessed our official betrothal."

Before Adam could reply, King Nicholas stood. "May this union be blessed with many heirs," he said. Again the crowd cheered, the orchestra began a joyous tune and Adam stared at Isabel in shocked surprise.

"What have you done?" he asked.

She raised her chin, a stubborn light adorning her gorgeous eyes. "I did what I had to do to get what I want." Again she took his hand and led him off the dance floor and out the door that led to the veranda.

Once there, she looked at him, her heart in her

eyes. "I let you go years ago because of duty. I knew you'd never allow yourself to love me as long as you had no closure where your father was concerned, so I hired those investigators to help you in your search for the truth."

Her eyes darkened. "I thought when I brought you that news, it would free your heart for me."

He touched the side of her face with his fingertips. "And I shoved you unceremoniously out the door."

She nodded. "I thought for sure there was no chance for us after that, that you didn't love me the same way I loved you."

"I needed some time alone, to say a final goodbye to my father," he explained. "And I still believed your father would dictate the man you would marry, and he would be of royal blood with titles and riches to match." He looked at her curiously. "How did you know your brother and your father would approve of me?"

"I wasn't worried about Nicholas. Nicholas performed the same ceremony with Rebecca and I knew Nicholas knows the value of true love."

"What about your father?"

"When I realized my father was stepping down from the throne to spend more time with my mother, I knew he wouldn't be a problem. He, too, has become aware of the treasure of love and family." She stepped closer to him. "So, are you mad at me? Do you want to be engaged to me?"

"No."

Her eyes widened and a tiny gasp escaped from her lips.

He smiled and gathered her into his arms. "I don't want to be engaged to you, Princess Isabel. I want to be married to you. I want to spend the rest of my life with you."

"Oh, Adam." Her eyes grew luminous with tears of happiness and when she raised her lips to his, he didn't hesitate.

He kissed her with fiery passion, with all the love and desire that burned inside of him for her. She returned the kiss with a fire and heat all her own.

"I hope you're agreeable to a short engagement," he said half-breathless when their kiss finally ended.

"A very short engagement," she replied. She grinned. "I guess this means Bella and Adam's divorce is off."

"Bella and Adam are going to be married for years to come," he replied. "They are going to have a houseful of children, a life filled with dreams and hearts filled with love."

"I love you, Lieutenant Commander," she said as her arms curled around his neck.

"And I love you, Princess," Adam replied, then he captured her lips once again, sealing the future in a kiss of everlasting love.

Epilogue

King Nicholas moved quietly through the darkened, silent chapel, a wiggling LeAnn in one arm, a flashlight in the other. Although he was exhausted, the excitement of the day still filled him with adrenaline.

When Isabel's and Adam's wedding had finally ended, he'd gone into the nursery to check on his baby girl. He'd expected to find her sound asleep, but she'd greeted him with giggles and the wide-eyed expression of a little girl not close to slumber.

He'd picked her up and cuddled her close, then had decided to take her with him. Behind the altar, he went down the stairs that led to the catacombs beneath the city.

The flashlight easily lit the narrow corridor he

followed and as he walked, LeAnn giggled at the dancing shadows they made on the walls.

He hugged her closer, loving the scent of sweet little girl, of his daughter. She was the child of his heart, born from the tremendous love Nicholas felt for LeAnn's mother. He had seen that same love pass between Isabel and Adam as they took their vows earlier that day. Isabel's face glowed and her perfectly fitted bridal gown made her look more like a princess than ever before.

He'd gone only a little ways when he stopped in front of an ornate fresco. The vivid colors had faded over time, but even the passing of centuries couldn't diminish the power and mastery of the work.

Nicholas looked down at the new ring that adorned his right hand. It was a large ring with an intricate center stone. The king's ring. His father had passed it to him the same afternoon when he'd passed him the reins of the country, before the coronation had begun.

It took him only a moment to locate the slight depression in the stone that his father had described to him. He pressed the front of his ring into the depression. Awe swept through him as the stone swung backward to reveal a secret chamber.

The Chamber of Riches.

How ironic it was that his father had been held only a hundred feet or so from here. The kidnappers had no idea how close they were to discovering the secret location of the Chamber of Riches.

Nicholas reached along the wall and found the switch that shot life into dozens of battery-powered lights. The room lit with a brilliance heightened only by the riches it contained.

As Nicholas stepped through the doorway, the stone slid silently back into place, closing him inside and hiding the room from anyone who might wander into the catacomb's corridor.

LeAnn reached for a jeweled tiara, then for a glittering ruby-encrusted set of candlesticks.

"Isn't it beautiful, LeAnn?" Nicholas said to his daughter. "And if your mother and I have our way, this will all be yours to keep for the future of Edenbourg."

LeAnn clapped her hands, as if she understood his words. He smiled as she wriggled her body and yawned. He lifted her so that her soft, downy head rested on his shoulder. "And I hope that when the day comes that this is yours, you'll understand that the real treasure of life can't be found in a hidden room or a Chamber of Riches."

Nicholas thought of Rebecca, his beautiful wife, the keeper of his dreams and the queen of his heart. He patted his daughter's little back. "I hope when the time comes you'll be wise enough to know that the real treasure can only be found in your heart and that treasure is love."

He opened the door of the Chamber of Riches and shut off the lights. As he walked back up the stairs to the chapel, he prayed that he would be a good king, but mostly he gave thanks for knowing that he had become a wealthy man the day he'd met his wife. Rebecca and LeAnn were all the treasure he needed.

* * * * *

Look for Carla Cassidy's book,

BORN OF PASSION,

part of Silhouette Intimate Moments'
brand-new continuity,
FIRST BORN SONS,
in August, 2001.

Feel like a star with Silhouette.

We will fly you and a guest to New York City for an exciting weekend stay at a glamorous 5-star hotel. Experience a refreshing day at one of New York's trendiest spas and have your photo taken by a professional. Plus, receive $1,000 U.S. spending money!

Flowers...long walks...dinner for two... how does Silhouette Books make romance come alive for you?

Send us a script, with 500 words or less, along with visuals (only drawings, magazine cutouts or photographs or combination thereof). Show us how Silhouette Makes Your Love Come Alive. Be creative and have fun. No purchase necessary. All entries must be clearly marked with your name, address and telephone number. All entries will become property of Silhouette and are not returnable. **Contest closes September 28, 2001.**

Please send your entry to: **Silhouette Makes You a Star!**

In U.S.A.
P.O. Box 9069
Buffalo, NY, 14269-9069

In Canada
P.O. Box 637
Fort Erie, ON, L2A 5X3

Look for contest details on the next page, by visiting www.eHarlequin.com or request a copy by sending a self-addressed envelope to the applicable address above. Contest open to Canadian and U.S. residents who are 18 or over. Void where prohibited.

Our lucky winner's photo will appear in a Silhouette ad. Join the fun!

SRMYAS1

HARLEQUIN "SILHOUETTE MAKES YOU A STAR!" CONTEST 1308
OFFICIAL RULES
NO PURCHASE NECESSARY TO ENTER

1. To enter, follow directions published in the offer to which you are responding. Contest begins June 1, 2001, and ends on September 28, 2001. Entries must be postmarked by September 28, 2001, and received by October 5, 2001. Enter by hand-printing (or typing) on an 8 ½" x 11" piece of paper your name, address (including zip code), contest number/name and attaching a script containing <u>500 words or less, along with drawings, photographs or magazine cutouts, or combinations thereof</u> (i.e., collage) <u>on no larger than 9" x 12"</u> piece of paper, describing how the <u>Silhouette books make romance come alive for you.</u> Mail via first-class mail to: Harlequin "Silhouette Makes You a Star!" Contest 1308, (in the U.S.) P.O. Box 9069, Buffalo, NY 14269-9069, (in Canada) P.O. Box 637, Fort Erie, Ontario, Canada L2A 5X3. Limit one entry per person, household or organization.

2. Contests will be judged by a panel of members of the Harlequin editorial, marketing and public relations staff. Fifty percent of criteria will be judged against script and fifty percent will be judged against drawing, photographs and/or magazine cutouts. Judging criteria will be based on the following:

   - Sincerity—25%
   - Originality and Creativity—50%
   - Emotionally Compelling—25%

In the event of a tie, duplicate prizes will be awarded. Decisions of the judges are final.

3. All entries become the property of Torstar Corp. and may be used for future promotional purposes. Entries will not be returned. No responsibility is assumed for lost, late, illegible, incomplete, inaccurate, nondelivered or misdirected mail.

4. Contest open only to residents of the U.S. (<u>except Puerto Rico</u>) and Canada who are 18 years of age or older, and is void wherever prohibited by law; all applicable laws and regulations apply. Any litigation within the Province of Quebec respecting the conduct or organization of a publicity contest may be submitted to the Régie des alcools, des courses et des jeux for a ruling. Any litigation respecting the awarding of a prize may be submitted to the Régie des alcools, des courses et des jeux only for the purpose of helping the parties reach a settlement. Employees and immediate family members of Torstar Corp. and D. L. Blair, Inc., their affiliates, subsidiaries and all other agencies, entities and persons connected with the use, marketing or conduct of this contest are not eligible to enter. Taxes on prizes are the sole responsibility of the winner. Acceptance of any prize offered constitutes permission to use winner's name, photograph or other likeness for the purposes of advertising, trade and promotion on behalf of Torstar Corp., its affiliates and subsidiaries without further compensation to the winner, unless prohibited by law.

5. Winner will be determined no later than November 30, 2001, and will be notified by mail. Winner will be required to sign and return an Affidavit of Eligibility/Release of Liability/Publicity Release form within 15 days after winner notification. Noncompliance within that time period may result in disqualification and an alternative winner may be selected. All travelers must execute a Release of Liability prior to ticketing and must possess required travel documents (e.g., passport, photo ID) where applicable. Trip must be booked by December 31, 2001, and completed within one year of notification. No substitution of prize permitted by winner. Torstar Corp. and D. L. Blair, Inc., their parents, affiliates and subsidiaries are not responsible for errors in printing of contest, entries and/or game pieces. In the event of printing or other errors that may result in unintended prize values or duplication of prizes, all affected game pieces or entries shall be null and void. **Purchase or acceptance of a product offer does not improve your chances of winning.**

6. Prizes: (1) Grand Prize—A 2-night/3-day trip for two (2) to New York City, including round-trip coach air transportation nearest winner's home and hotel accommodations (double occupancy) at The Plaza Hotel, a glamorous afternoon makeover at <u>a trendy New York spa</u>, $1,000 in U.S. spending money and an opportunity to <u>have a professional photo taken and appear in a Silhouette advertisement</u> (approximate retail value: $7,000). (10) Ten Runner-Up Prizes of gift packages (retail value $50 ea.). Prizes consist of only those items listed as part of the prize. Limit one prize per person. Prize is valued in U.S. currency.

7. For the name of the winner (available after December 31, 2001) send a self-addressed, stamped envelope to: Harlequin "Silhouette Makes You a Star!" Contest 1197 Winners, P.O. Box 4200 Blair, NE 68009-4200 or you may access the www.eHarlequin.com Web site through February 28, 2002.

Contest sponsored by Torstar Corp., P.O Box 9042, Buffalo, NY 14269-9042.

SRMYAS2